Wh‍‍‍ng

4 Stars!

"...Michelle creates every woman's vampire fantasy with a hero who is dark, brooding and dangerous, not to mention an exceptional lover. Rana is the perfect foil with her bright outlook on life and sensitive nature. Rana and Lucian must make decisions that alter their lives, all in the name of love.

- Pamela Cohen for Romantic Times Book Club Magazine

"...Ms. Michelle is definitely an author on the rise and one not to be missed. I personally look forward to more work from this amazing author who knows how to grab her readers attention from page one and to bring us characters that we will think about for a long time to come..."

-Tracey West for The Road to Romance

"...Emotional, tender, sensual, sweet, funny, suspenseful, erotic, joyful – these are all words that describe this book..."

-Missy Andrews for Romance Junkies Review

"...A TASTE FOR PASSION is a wonderful, hot, sexy read. For a second novel, Ms. Michelle really shows her writing skills. Lucian is an alpha male who is great vampire. Rana's softness and sensitivity make her the perfect match for Lucian. The tension is great throughout the story; it will keep you on the edge of your seat. I would love to see a story about the secondary characters. A great read, you won't be disappointed."

-Patricia McGrew for Sensual Romance

Discover for yourself why readers can't get enough of the multiple award-winning publisher Ellora's Cave. Whether you prefer e-books or paperbacks, be sure to visit EC on the web at www.ellorascave.com for an erotic reading experience that will leave you breathless.

www.ellorascave.com

Ellora's Cave Publishing, Inc.
PO Box 787
Hudson, OH 44236-0787

ISBN # 1-84360-569-4

A TASTE FOR PASSION, 2003.
ALL RIGHTS RESERVED
Ellora's Cave Publishing, Inc.
© A TASTE FOR PASSION, Patrice Michelle, 2003.

This book may not be reproduced in whole or in part without author and publisher permission.

Editing by Martha Punches.
Cover art by Dawn Seewer.

Warning: The following material contains strong sexual content meant for mature readers. A TASTE FOR PASSION has been rated Borderline NC17 erotic, by a minimum of three independent reviewers. We strongly suggest storing this book in a place where young readers not meant to view it are unlikely to happen upon it. That said, enjoy…

A TASTE FOR PASSION

by

PATRICE MICHELLE

Also by Patrice Michelle:

- Bad In Boots: Harm's Hunger

Chapter One

Rana pressed hard on the pedal and flinched when the engine made an unmistakable revving whine. She gripped the gearshift and shoved it into fifth gear.

What are you trying to do, Rana, kill her? She could practically hear Jack groaning at the sound. How she wished her grandfather were here to needle her.

Tears streamed down her face. "Well, I wouldn't be driving your damn precious 'Vette in the first place if you were still alive, old man," she muttered under her breath. All the pain poured out in a new flood of tears.

Late afternoon sun lit her path as wide-open roads greeted her; dirt flew behind the wheels as the speedometer hit seventy and continued to climb.

She shifted to the last gear, reveling at the sense of total control the extra gear gave her. The 'Vette's engine kicked in, purring beneath her. Rana hit the button on the door. The electric window whirred down and wind rushed in, whipping through her hair. She closed her eyes for a second and tried to imagine how her flamboyant grandfather might feel with the car's power rumbling underneath him. She opened her eyes as a brief smile formed on her lips at the passing thought—he probably got his jollies. Rana ignored the farmhouses and prairies that sped past, a blur of colors and country smells, and punched the pedal to the floor, seeking a connection with her grandfather.

Gripping the wheel with both hands as the 'Vette hugged a sharp curve, she recalled her parent's shocked faces as she'd sped off in Jack's car, remembered Mother's warm smile and worried eyes when she handed Rana the letter.

"Since you were so upset during the funeral, I thought I'd wait a little while before I gave you this."

Her grandfather's letter would forever be burned in her memory.

Rana,

I love you with all my heart. I'll always be with you. I want you to have my 'Vette. Drive her, Rana, my girl. Taste the passion life has to offer. Spend every day as if it were your last. You never know what tomorrow will bring.

Love, Jack

She drove endlessly, mindless of her destination. Eventually, the landscape changed and narrowed as thick trees lined both sides of the road, darkening her path. The sun barely made it through the canopy of dense foliage.

Rana flicked on the headlights and glanced up in shock at the deer that bounded ahead, stopping not twenty feet in front of her. She hit the brakes. The car jerked, fishtailed and started to spin. Loose dirt flew up around her. The 'Vette continued its 360 degree rotation. Rana locked her grip on the wheel, closed her eyes, and waited for the inevitable collision. *Hope you got the chessboard ready, Jack. I'm about to join you.*

Finally, with one last lurch, the car stopped, the engine still alive, rumbling beneath her. She looked up, her heart thudding in her chest. The smell of burned rubber assailed her and she coughed. When the cloud of dust settled, she met the deer's stare before it bounded away, unharmed.

"I could've died," she whispered, gripping the steering wheel so tight, her hands turned numb. Her breath came in little hysterical pants and her body trembled all over at the near miss. "I could've died."

Flashes of memories tore through her mind: Jack's eyes alight with victory as he said, 'Checkmate', Jack waggling his eyebrows after a single woman at a neighborhood picnic, Jack throwing a surprise keg party for her when she graduated from college—she ended up driving *him* home.

She lifted her head and stared at the roof, calling out in frustration and anger, "How could you leave me like this? You're my best friend, remember? I expected us to have at least twenty more years together. We made a great team. I kept you grounded and you helped me fly."

She knew it didn't make much sense. He had been old, even if he didn't act it, or look it. She trailed off and lowered her gaze, her image in the rearview mirror capturing her attention. Taking in her hazel green eyes and dark blond hair, she gave a short laugh, followed by a hiccup. They couldn't have been more opposite.

Whereas her looks were mediocre at best, even at seventy, Jack had aged well. She could just picture him on the front of a GQ magazine in his stylish clothes—that devil-may-care smile pasted on his face. He didn't just live his life, he welcomed each day with a challenging gleam in his eyes. From the car he drove, to his friendly nature, Jack was all flash, an extrovert extraordinaire. He even insisted she call him Jack instead of Grandfather.

Her mother had written her paternal parent off long ago, but not Rana. She loved her grandfather fiercely. So what if the man had been through his first mid-life crisis at forty and two wives later — the first lost to a divorce, the second to cancer — he's tooling around in his electric blue Corvette, looking for wife number three? And that's how Jack died — experiencing life to the fullest — in a hotel room with a woman half his age.

How many times had he said to her with that wicked grin, "Girl, you gotta get out there and let people get to know the real Rana. That wit of yours will keep 'em on their toes." Her personality had always been more reserved, especially around people she didn't know.

Rana smiled bitterly. *Well, that was the thing, Jack. You were the 'yang' to my 'yin'. You drew me out, made me better than I was.*

Jack may have had his faults, but the one thing he had always done well was look out for her. For twenty-eight years he'd been her friend, her confidant, her advisor. Jack thrived in that role, especially the advice-giving part. He loved to give advice, or better yet, his opinion. "Rana, my girl, you need a man in your life."

Yep, finding her a boyfriend had been his latest campaign, to which she had replied with a laugh, "But I have you."

With the opening of her bookstore last year, Rana had been too busy with advertising, setting up inventory, and working with vendors to think about a boyfriend. *Man, when was the last time I had sex? Uh-uh, don't go there or you'll just be more depressed.*

Now, she was alone. She hated being alone.

Rana swiped away her tears and tried to shake off her melancholy mood. Knowing Jack wouldn't want her to mourn, she turned the car around and headed back to the city. Off in the distance, Chicago's skyline pierced the pink and purple sky, beckoning her return.

As she reached the outskirts of town, she called her parents on her cell phone to let them know she wasn't dead in some ditch—yet—and snapped the phone closed. Looking up, she saw a bright yellow sign set back from the road. 'Antiques for Sale,' it read in bold black letters. Rana's passion, second only to books, was antiquing. Making a last minute decision, she turned her car down the long driveway toward the shop.

You're nuts. One minute you're crying, the next you're antiquing.

No, Rana my girl, you're finally getting it right. Life's too short. Taste the passion. She heard Jack's spirited voice in her head.

Okay, Jack, I know you had some psychic ability when you were alive, but I can't believe you're that good.

As Rana parked her car, she realized with a smile Jack's voice in her head was her way of holding on to his memory. The thought gave her strength.

A bell above the door rang out when she entered the small, cramped shop. Turn-of- the-century furniture filled the picture window: a red velvet sofa with gold piping trimmed with tassels, a hand-carved Italian chestnut chair with dragon arms, and a small Pietra Dura end table with a black marble top. More furniture, lamps, rugs and pictures took up every nook and cranny of the shop.

"Hello there." A willowy figure approached from the back of the store. As the woman stepped out of the shadows, the late afternoon sun steaming through the picture window shone on her face, which caused her to squint and retreat. She made a tsking sound and whipped out a pair of sunglasses from her denim jacket pocket, placing them on her nose.

She smiled and stepped closer. "There, that's better. What are you looking for today, my dear?"

Rana stared at her, transfixed. The woman looked to be in her mid-thirties with raven black hair and flawless fair skin. She stood a good three inches taller than Rana's own five-foot seven-inch frame. Her eyes, before she'd covered them, were an unusual shade of lavender, reminding Rana of tanzanite.

Shaking her head, Rana answered, "I'm just looking today." She gave a sheepish smile and remembering her swollen eyes and tear-stained face, quickly wiped her cheeks with her palms. "I like antiquing."

The woman smiled her understanding and put out her hand. "I'm Sabryn."

Rana shook her hand. "My name's Rana."

She walked around the shop, lifting picture frames, opening drawers.

Sabryn called out from behind the counter. "I have some antique jewelry. Would you like to peruse it as well?"

Fingering her grandmother's white gold locket around her neck, Rana laughed. "I'd love to. I adore jewelry."

She pulled out a velvet-lined drawer and laid it on the case's glass top.

Rana walked over to the counter and gasped at the display of earrings, necklaces and rings. "Oh, they're beautiful." She touched a silver ring, glancing up. "May I?"

Sabryn smiled. "Of course."

Pulling the ring out of its holder, Rana slipped it on her third finger. A nostalgic sense of belonging gripped her, causing her to inhale deeply.

"See, it was made just for you." Sabryn leaned forward, looking at her hand.

Moving her hand toward the sunlight, Rana wiggled her fingers. The warm rays caught the facets on the chips of silver stones covering the half-inch wide band, making her smile. The pure color saturation of the two blood-red teardrop-shaped gemstones flanking either side of the pear-shaped cutout sold her on the ring. Rana touched the bare area at the top of the ring saying, "It's almost as if the ring wasn't finished."

Sabryn leaned over once more, eyeing the ring. "Mmmm, I see what you mean." She straightened, indicating the tray of jewelry. "You can pick something else, if you like."

Rana pulled her hand back and curled her fingers into an involuntary fist. She laughed. "No, I like this one. How old is it? The style is unusual."

"It's about seventy years old."

"How much?" She was almost afraid to ask.

"Four hundred."

Yikes. But I have to have it. At least the folks at Visa will be dancing a happy jig. "I'll take it." Rana retrieved her credit card and tried not to wince as Sabryn rang it up. "I like your perfume, by the way."

Sabryn shook her head and gave her a smile. "I'm not wearing any."

"You aren't?" Rana was taken aback. The lavender-like smell was so distinct. Where was it coming from?

"No, but thanks anyway."

She pulled out a box, but Rana waved her hand. "No need. I want to wear it."

Sabryn put the box away and handed her the receipt to sign.

When she turned to leave the shop, Sabryn called after her, "Enjoy your ring, dear."

Rana returned home at a more leisurely — translated, less insane — pace. The trip to the antique shop had done the trick. She felt better. Jack might have gotten a kick out of seeing her put the pedal to the metal in his 'Vette, but he wouldn't want his gift to make her cry.

* * * * *

"What's your name?" Rana approached the dark-haired man. A misty haze surrounded him, forcing her to focus on his tall frame. His long black trench coat flapped in the crisp fall wind as he stared at her with silver eyes.

He didn't answer, but instead asked, "Do I know you?" A slight smile lifted the corners of his lips.

Rana squirmed under his close scrutiny. She wasn't usually so forward with men she didn't know.

"Yes," she blurted out. "Um, I mean, no."

He raised an eyebrow. "So which is it, yes or no?"

Rana's cheeks grew hot at his amused expression. "Well, I…I don't know," she stammered.

Her heart hammered as he placed his hands on her arms and pulled her to him, his lips close to hers. "Then let me remind you."

This man's kiss wasn't a tentative, I-want-to-get-to-know-you brush of the lips. Oh, no. It was an all-out, soul searching, I've-tasted-every-last-inch-of-your-body-and-know-just-how-you-like-it kiss — the kind that flashed right down to her toes and burned right back up, hitting all the right buttons. Her thighs trembled, her stomach clenched, and her breasts ached for his touch.

Rana's hands landed on his chest for support. The unyielding muscular surface underneath the soft leather of his coat sent a thrill zipping down her spine. Her sex throbbed as his tongue danced with hers. He slid his hands inside her coat, clasped her waist and pulled her against him — hard chest to soft breast, narrow hips to flared ones. His heart beating against her chest made a deeper connection with her and her own heart rate stuttered, slowing until it met his steady rhythm. He cupped his hands on the curve of her rear end and pressed his erection against her. Her breasts tingled as his heat soaked right through her jeans.

"You feel so good," he rasped while his lips skimmed the edge of her jaw line and dipped lower. He laid a kiss in the hollow of her throat and worked his way to the sensitive flesh just below her left ear.

Liquid heat rushed south. The achy sensation made her moan and rub against him, seeking release from the pulsing pressure. Rana threaded her fingers into his thick hair as he kissed her neck. "I could say the same about you," she replied with a sigh as his teeth grazed her throat.

Sliding his leg between hers, he pressed against her sex and gave a growl of satisfaction. "Your heat attracts me." He trailed his warm tongue down her throat and continued, "But your scent seduces me."

Rana smiled at his words and gasped in pleasure when he clamped his teeth lightly on her neck, tightened his grip on her buttocks, and rubbed his long, muscular thigh against her cleft as he pulled her up his leg.

She let out a cry at the glorious friction, amazed that he knew just what to do to make her body sing. She heard the cool wind whisk around them, but Rana didn't feel it, her body thrummed with its own inner fire.

He stopped his movements and held her against his leg, suspended off the ground, teetering on the edge of her climax, totally at his mercy. God, she'd beg him if she had to.

"Look at me."

Rana met his intense gaze, panting, clinging to his shoulders.

"Remember us," he insisted and yanked her up his leg, flush against his chest.

She screamed and her blood pressure skyrocketed as her body shook all over from her highly charged orgasm.

Rana sat up with a gasp and then slumped back in sexual frustration, slamming her hand on the cushioned arm of the chair—the book she had been reading slid off her lap to the floor with a thump. "Well, nuts! Great job, Rana, waking up from your nap before the ripping-clothes-off-hot-n'-sweaty-naked-bodies-scene came next."

Her heart still thudding in her chest, a dull ache between her thighs, she sat back and thought about the one and only time she'd seen the man from her dream.

Jack's funeral had hit her hard. She remembered sitting there, numb all over as the first clumps of dirt hit his coffin with a resounding thump. He's gone. The second handful made a dull, muted thud. No more chess games. The third made no sound at all. No more jokes. Her mother spoke to her. But she shook her head, unable to hear, unable to comprehend that her grandfather was gone.

She'd lingered in solitude by the graveside after her family and other mourners had filed away to their cars. No sounds penetrated her mind—all she heard was her own shallow breathing. She realized she was in shock, denial, whatever the word.

She had to force herself to walk away, but unable to resist, she took one last enduring look back, her heart breaking. Her eyes closed, shutting out the vision and then opened again as she turned away, her entire body moving in slow motion.

As she exited the cemetery, she was so caught up in her grief, she didn't notice anyone else until she accidentally rubbed shoulders with someone entering. In that one moment, all her senses came slamming back, stronger than they'd ever been. The late afternoon sun had disappeared behind the clouds, making the fall air crisper as it cut into her coat. She noted the scent of chimney fires smelled stronger and the sound of hands patting backs as friends hugged her family members sounded more distinct. She inhaled a deep breath at the sensory overload and glanced over her shoulder at the stranger as she continued walking.

The tall man had turned his head too. He stopped walking and faced her. Since he wore sunglasses, she couldn't see his eyes, but she saw his brows draw together behind the dark frames as if he were studying her. Sudden, unexpected awareness rushed through her. He seemed...familiar.

Her mother put her arm around her, pulling her toward the car and away from her distracted thoughts. "Are you okay, honey?"

That had been a week ago. Rana sat straight up in the chair when she realized Mr. Tall, Dark, and Seductive from her dream had had silver-blue eyes. But the man in the cemetery had worn sunglasses. How could she have made up such an unusual eye color?

She sat back with an ironic half smile. If she ever did get to meet the man from her dream in person, she could hear Jack now, taking credit, even from the grave. *Yep, got those two together, I sure did.*

* * * * *

"Lucian, the evening has arrived."

"Oh, Luuuucian."

"Lucian, wake up!"

Lucian came out of his self-induced deep sleep to find Sabryn and his Uncle Vlad leaning over him.

Sabryn frowned slightly. "Get up, brother. It is time for you to feed."

Lucian stretched his rested body and gave them a lazy smile. "To what do I owe this honor, you two?"

Sabryn paced away from his bed. "'Tis not normal, you sleep so much, Lucian. You must feed. You must take your place as leader of the vampires in five days. Father has been gone for two years now. Even though our bylaws state a period of mourning is required before the seat is filled, the chair has remained unclaimed too long." She faced him, her cheeks rosy in her frustration. "Kraid will challenge you for the position."

Lucian sat up and scrubbed his hands over his face. "Really, Sabryn, you're making too much of this." He waved his hand dismissively. "I know Kantrue's have usually led the vampires, but I don't know if I want to take the Vité position."

Accepting the role meant he'd have to be constantly available for the council meetings or to make decisions related to the five clans he'd oversee. He wouldn't be able to retreat into his own world as he'd done the last few years.

Both Sabryn and Uncle Vlad faced him, saying in unison, "You must, Lucian."

Lucian narrowed his eyes on them. "What's going on? Why are you two so uptight?"

Vlad glided toward him and stood beside the bed. "Lucian, while you have slept the 'deep sleep' these past two months, some of the vampires in Kraid's Bruen clan have killed humans, a couple of them violently. We believe he's not doing enough to curb this behavior."

"Ha!" Sabryn folded her arms over her chest and tossed her long black hair over her shoulder. "He's not doing anything. I think he condones it. It's no secret he believes humans are an inferior race."

Lucian stood up, anger bubbling within him. Lightheadedness rewarded his hasty movements. Kraid's stupidity could expose them all. There were many humans he called friends, but how would they feel about him if they knew he was a vampire? "Where is Kraid now?" he said quietly.

Sabryn put her hand on his tense arm. "Lucian, no, you must feed first, regain your strength. You've been too long without sustenance. You'd be no match for Kraid in your condition."

Lucian pressed his lips together in frustration, but he knew his sister was right. While neither she nor his uncle knew about his secret visits to Elizabeth's grave, it had been a week since he'd last fed. He nodded and started to shimmer into mist.

"Wait," Sabryn called. Lucian turned back to her, his eyebrow raised. She smiled. "I want to hunt with you tonight, brother." *There's something we need to discuss,* she whispered in his mind.

His uncle raised his brow. They both knew Sabryn preferred to hunt alone. But he didn't say a word, even though Lucian knew the curiosity was killing him.

Lucian grabbed her hand and smiled. "It'll be like when we were children."

Sabryn laughed and shimmered into mist right along with him.

* * * * *

Lucian leaned against his Jaguar outside his nightclub, The Lion's Lair, as he waited for Sabryn to feed. He shook his head and gave a low chuckle. Sabryn didn't have to use her ability to compel the man. One kiss from her sultry lips and a man willingly offered her his neck. She approached with a smile on her lips.

"Are you going to at least let him remember your name this time?" Lucian asked, amusement reflected in his tone.

She widened her smile, showing him her fangs before she let them retract back to their normal size. "Just because you choose not to erase your presence doesn't mean I have to."

Lucian shook his head. "Are you ever going to let yourself get close to anyone, Sabryn?"

His sister stiffened. "No, not ever again."

Lucian put his hand on her shoulder. "I'm sorry. But it's been fifty years. Surely, you can move on."

Sabryn shrugged his hand off her shoulder. "I'm not here to talk about me. Now that you've fed, we have much to discuss."

Lucian folded his arms over his chest, decidedly curious. "Do go on."

She gave him a knowing smile. "You know how you've put Elizabeth's ring in jeweler's windows in hopes she'd return to you one day?"

Lucian's entire body tensed. He didn't dare hope. He dropped his arms, his breath escaping in a whisper. "Yes."

"Well, I'll bet you didn't know I stole it, did you?"

He fisted his hands by his sides. "You what?" he thundered. Seventy years ago, he lost his fiancée, Elizabeth, in a riding accident before he could make her his bride and a vampire, too. Depression set in for months until his uncle reminded him of the circle of life and his belief in reincarnation.

Lucian clung to the concept, his only hope. Over the years he'd sought out jewelers, befriending them and asked them to display Elizabeth's ring—a ring he'd personally made for his love—in his or her shop window. He clung to the belief that Elizabeth would find him.

As decades passed, he realized his dreams were nothing more than wishful thinking and the loneliness became too much to bear. The realization he'd never find his mate, coupled with his father's death, was why he'd taken to hibernating in recent months.

Sabryn gave him an indignant look. "It was a work of art and worth more than what you're allowing your jeweler friends to sell it for. I thought to put it in my shop." She raised her chin haughtily. "At least among antiquities, it would be appreciated for what it was."

Lucian snorted. "Yeah, among little old, blue-haired ladies. I might be older than them, but my tastes run a bit younger, Sabryn."

"How would you know the woman that bought your ring was Elizabeth reincarnated?"

He eyed her, not sure of her intent, but answered her anyway. "Because she would be attracted to the scent the ring emanates, a scent only she could detect."

She smiled. "A human woman bought your ring today."

He sent her a doubtful look.

Sabryn's smile broadened, her eyes shining as she swept her arm wide. "Let the wind help you find her, brother. Her name is Rana Sterling."

Lucian put his hands on her shoulders, clasping them tight. "Sabryn, don't toy with me."

She laid her palm on his cheek, a sincere tone in her words. "I'm not, Lucian. She commented on my perfume—that she liked it." She grinned. "I wasn't wearing any."

Lucian shifted into a raven's form before she finished the last word, leaving his clothes behind in a heap on the ground. His sister's melodious laughter floated behind him as he soared to the sky. The sound made his heart sing. *Yes, dear sister, now I too have a reason to laugh.*

Chapter Two

Lucian flew for hours, concentrating all his efforts on his keen sense of smell. But unfortunately it had rained earlier in the evening and he couldn't catch a scent. He returned to the deserted parking lot, disappointed, but not discouraged. It was only a matter of time. He'd find her.

Once he'd slid on his discarded clothes, he walked inside the nearly empty nightclub. It was almost time to close up. Ian flagged him down at the bar.

As Lucian approached the bar, he had to chuckle. Contrary to Hollywood's popular portrayal, vampires might not eat, but they certainly drank. After all, living for centuries would be pretty boring if they couldn't relax every once in a while.

Lucian ordered a drink and a phonebook, and settled beside his childhood friend. He smiled in reminiscence at all they'd gone through together over the years.

"It's been too long, my friend." Ian clapped him on the shoulder. His calm, golden eyes searched Lucian's as a grin rode up his face.

"Something seems different about you." Ian rubbed his jaw thoughtfully and then dropped his hand, his eyebrows lifting in anticipation. "You're going to take your father's place, aren't you?"

Lucian took a sip of his whiskey. "I have something I need to do first."

"Sabryn told me she mentioned the murders to you. Kraid killed a human as well, not just the two vamps under him." Ian ran a hand through his short, tawny hair, his frustration evident.

Lucian set his jaw at the news. He trusted his friend to know the facts. Ian was a member of Kraid's Bruen clan. In all his years, he had never seen a more divided group. The Bruen clan was made up of two types of men: the loud, arrogant, angry ones and the idealists. There was no room for those that fell right in the middle.

Ian was one of those men—wild and a bit rough around the edges, but strong, self-assured, true to his word, and loyal to the Kindred first and foremost. Well, loyal until a vamp crossed the line. After that, Ian was the first one to rein the transgressor in. He didn't give a damn that he didn't fit an expected Bruen mould. Lucian's lips curved into a smile. And that's exactly what the Bruen clan needed in a leader—someone who didn't take sides and would keep the vamps on the straight and narrow.

"If I take the position of Vité, I want you to lead the Bruens."

"What?" Ian choked on his beer. He turned wide eyes his way and shook his head. "I'm too blunt to be a smooth talking leader, Luc."

Lucian faced his friend. "There's no one I trust more."

"I think Kraid might have something to say about that." Ian gave a low chuckle.

Lucian pinned him with a serious stare. "You're not afraid of Kraid are you?"

"Hell, no." Ian shot back.

Lucian held back his grin. He knew his old friend way too well. "I'll probably kill Kraid myself before this is all over." And that would be a welcomed transition after years of biding his time. "But if he bolts, I trust you'll hunt him down."

"It'll be my pleasure." Ian lifted his beer in salute, a wicked gleam in his eyes.

Lucian knew he meant it. Ian and Kraid had never seen eye-to-eye. The only person he despised more was Kraid's brother, Drace.

Ian inspired either confidence or respectful tolerance in all who knew him. His reputation as a relentless hunter of rogue vampires had earned him quite a nickname. He'd heard some call his friend Ian the Enforcer. Because of the human blood that ran in his veins, the sun didn't affect him. That fact alone made him a considerable adversary.

Satisfied that he'd set his plans in motion, Lucian flipped through the phonebook and searched the listings under Sterling. What if Rana was married? He shook off the fear that gripped him. No. He knew in his heart she wouldn't be.

"Whatcha' doing?" Ian tapped the book with his beer bottle.

"Trying to locate a woman." Lucian looked up. "Her name is Rana Sterling."

Ian chuckled. "Well it's about damn time, Luc, my boy. I'd begun to worry about you."

Lucian grinned and shook his head, returning his gaze to the book. "She bought my ring today."

"No shit?" Ian sat up straight on his stool.

Sliding his finger down the row of Sterlings, Lucian memorized them, but there wasn't a Rana listed among them. Maybe Rana was a nickname, or her number was unlisted.

Sabryn breezed past, throwing a newspaper on the bar in front of him, and calling behind her, "Just wanted you to catch up on old news."

Lucian eyed his sister's retreating back. He knew what she was doing. She wanted to knock the guilt factor up a notch. He picked up the week old paper and read the front page news, the investigator's interpretation of what had happened to the victims. Apparently, wild dogs had mauled the bodies. But one corpse had also been drained of considerable blood, which made the police suspect some kind of ritualistic killing.

His anger rose, his normally slow heart beat faster as he catalogued the names of the victims and flipped to the obituary pages. An unsuspecting human didn't stand a chance against a vampire, especially a vampire who'd let his thirst turn to bloodlust. The least he could do was anonymously send flowers, even if belatedly, to the grieving families.

While he scanned the long list of names, his gaze landed and locked on an obituary.

> *Jack Rodgers was laid to rest today in Haven's Cemetery.*
>
> *He lived a long, full life and had no regrets. He is survived by his*
>
> *daughter and granddaughter, Jane and Rana Sterling.*

Lucian's heart pounded in his chest when he read her name. He knew, without a doubt, Rana was the woman from the cemetery, the same woman he'd had such an intense, unsettling reaction to.

His mind whirled. Her name wasn't listed among the Sterlings he'd memorized, but the curator of the funeral home should have her address or at least her phone number. He smiled and started to call for a phone when he realized it was four in the morning. He'd have to wait until at least eight to call.

"Hey, buddy. You okay?" Ian's voice came from far away. He waved his hand in front of him.

Lucian turned to his blood brother. "This is the important thing I need to do, Ian. I can't take the position without her."

"You have it bad, Luc." Ian shook his head. "Even after seventy years. Man, am I glad I never let a chick get under my skin the way you did with Elizabeth."

Lucian's neck grew hot at the flippant remark. He narrowed his eyes. Any other vamp would be dead for uttering such words in his presence, but Ian just looked at him with amusement in his eyes.

Smiling broadly, Lucian displayed his fangs. It was enough.

Ian sobered. "Sorry, Luc." He grinned sheepishly. "You know what I meant."

* * * * *

"Me?" Ian mouthed to the sexy redhead across the room while pointing to his chest.

She smiled, looked down at her mixed drink, and slowly swirled her stirrer in the ice.

Ian turned back to Lucian. "Hey, let me know if you need anything, okay?"

Lucian chuckled. "Go, Ian. I smell her arousal."

"I know." Ian grinned and slid off the stool to walk toward the woman.

"Hi," she said huskily as he approached and sat down beside her.

"Hey," he replied as he traced a finger down her bare arm. She watched the path his finger took and shivered when her green eyes met his.

"My name is Mona."

"Name's Ian," he said as the corners of his lips turned up at the lurid thoughts his mind associated with her name.

She gave him a sly smile as if she knew exactly what he was thinking. "Yes, I am well named."

Ian chuckled. "I see you and I are going to get along quite well."

"I thought your sexy friend would join us, too." She inclined her head toward the bar.

Lust surged through his body at her suggestion and he raised an eyebrow. "So you're into double-the-fun, are you?"

Mona dipped her finger in her drink and sucked the liquor off of the tip before she ran it along his bottom lip. "If it's with the right combination of men, then the answer is yes."

Ian captured her finger with his lips and sucked it inside his mouth, swirling his tongue around her flesh. His cock throbbed as he heard her heart rate pick up and her breathing turn shallow. He laced his fingers in hers and drew her hand down from his mouth. "Then don't worry, Mona, I've got just the right combination for you." He tugged gently on her hand. "Come on, let's get outta here."

Chapter Three

Ian stood outside his brother's loft apartment wondering at Duncan's mood. Mona leaned against his chest as he rang the doorbell.

When Duncan opened the door, Mona sucked in her breath in delight. Ian chuckled. Women always reacted that way when they saw the two brothers together.

"My God, I've never met a pair of twins that looked so much alike." She turned and stared at him and then looked back at Duncan.

Duncan stood there in a black turtleneck and black jeans, looking every bit the brooding loner he was. Whereas Ian embraced and reveled in his differences from other vampires, openly taunting them, Duncan withdrew, living a solitary life. The only person he remained close to over the years was his twin.

He leaned against the door jamb and addressed Ian, purposefully ignoring Mona. "To what do I owe the honor of your visit, Ian?"

Ian rubbed Mona's arms underneath her jacket. "Mona and I thought we'd come for a visit." *Be nice, Duncan. You need this.*

Being the first born, Ian felt a certain responsibility for his twin. It bothered him that his brother secluded himself from both humans and vampires. Duncan shared his ability to abide full sunlight but he also had a special power Ian didn't possess—a power that other vampires feared even more than the twins' ability to walk in daylight.

Duncan gave Ian a broad smile and Mona jumped back, gasping when she saw his fangs on full display.

"You—you're a vampire?" She leaned into Ian and jerked her gaze up to his face in shock, then pulled away from him, too when her mind made the 'identical twin' connection.

Anger surfacing at his brother's insolent stunt, Ian started to compel her, to alleviate her fear.

"Do not, brother," Duncan demanded.

Ian met his brother's gaze, letting his own reflect his irritation.

Duncan addressed Mona for the first time. "The idea that I will take your blood excites you, doesn't it, Mona Lisa?"

She nodded slowly and Ian caught the scent of her arousal once more. "How did you know my middle name?" she asked Duncan, a quizzical look on her heart shaped face.

Duncan gave her a secretive, sexy smile. Putting his hand out, he beckoned her, "Come inside and visit for a while."

Ian chuckled and followed Mona as she put her hand in Duncan's, allowing him to escort her inside. Personally, he didn't get into sharing, but he knew Duncan would refuse to be alone with her. Ian's desire to see his brother break free of his self-imposed seclusion overrode his own preferences. His brother *needed* to interact with humans, to get to know the other half of his heritage.

Duncan led Mona into the living room area and leaned against the fireplace mantle as she walked around the room. Ian took in the black leather couch and matching side chair set off by the silver and glass contemporary coffee table in his brother's living room. He wondered what Mona thought of his brother's taste.

She likes it. Duncan answered him mentally in a bored voice. *She thinks the combination fits my dangerous persona quite well.* He finished with a mental chuckle.

And that was the crux of the problem with his brother. Because of Duncan's special ability to read minds, humans were an open-book to him and therefore, boring. He didn't associate with them, seeing humans only as a source of food. Vampire's minds were strong, but their minds were susceptible to Duncan, too, if their guard was down. Therefore, male vampires gave Duncan a wide berth. The vampire women, on the other hand, flocked to him, drawn to the dangerous loner his twin had become. More often than not, he turned them away, too.

Then why don't you let her get to know the real you, Duncan? Ian watched Mona trail her fingers over Duncan's saxophone sitting in its stand against the wall.

Duncan met his gaze, his golden eyes so much like his own but more distant and intense than they should be. *She thinks it's intriguing that I play the sax, but she's not really interested in music. She's here for one reason.*

His brother turned to her and put out his hand, saying, "Come with me, Mona."

Duncan led Mona across the gleaming oak wood floor to the curved open staircase leading to his bedroom. Ian grinned as he slid his hand along the stair's chrome rail, following them. His brother certainly didn't waste any time.

When they entered his bedroom, Duncan flipped his hand and a fire suddenly raged in the black marble fireplace. Mona gasped at the sight. Ian just shook his head. Duncan, for all his varying moods, from brooding to somber, could really put on a show when he chose to.

While Mona stood in front of Duncan near the fireplace, Ian walked up behind her. He placed his hands on her hips and pulled her back against his hard erection. She made mewing sounds and rubbed her rear end closer. Ian gripped her hips tighter, the scent of her blood and arousal calling to him. Mona walked her fingers up Duncan's arms and started to put her arms around his neck, but he swiftly turned her around to face his brother. She sighed and wrapped her arms around Ian's neck.

Ian met his twin's unfathomable gaze before he pulled Mona closer and kissed her, delving his tongue into her mouth, tasting her, priming her as he slowly slid her coat off her shoulders and unbuttoned her red silk vest, revealing naked breasts underneath. Duncan unzipped her matching skirt and she wiggled her hips to help him remove the fabric along with her underwear.

Naked before them, Mona's head fell back as Ian cupped her breast in his hand and kissed a path down her throat, past the vein that beat rapidly in her neck. The fast rhythm of her pulse, such a beautiful sight to behold, beckoned to him. His nostrils flared as lust and raw hunger coalesced into an unfulfilled craving—the need for blood, for sustenance overpowering. He had to taste her.

Have you fed, brother? He silently asked Duncan.

Yes. Take your fill, Ian. Duncan turned to leave.

Mona looked puzzled and asked, "Aren't you staying, Duncan?"

"No, I'm going back downstairs."

Anger sliced through Ian at his brother's refusal to get to know Mona, to share something intimate with another person. *Duncan, I brought her for you.* He let his annoyance come across in his thoughts as he held his brother's gaze.

Yes, I know. Now enjoy my present, Ian. Duncan gave him an amused look before he walked out of the room.

Ian turned back to Mona. Cupping the back of her head, he kissed her as the first few notes of Duncan's saxophone reached his ears—the tune, at first, hip and upbeat, slipped into a slower melody. The melancholy, lonely solo made his heart ache for his brother. When he slid his hands down her sides and pulled her closer to deepen the kiss, Ian felt Duncan probing his mind as he had done all their lives. His brother's ability had always given him an advantage over Ian in the past, but Duncan was unaware Ian had learned to add layers to his thinking over the years.

Just below the surface of his consciousness, an idea formed, causing Ian to smile as his tongue traced a path down Mona's neck while he slid his fingers into the dark red curls between her legs. He wanted to feed her need as well as his own. Mona sighed her pleasure as his finger found her moist entrance and dove inside. The scent of her desire, the pounding of her blood throughout her veins, had his cock aching for release and his hunger raging within him.

When she gripped his shoulders and threw her head back as he rubbed against her clitoris, Ian couldn't hold back any longer. He kissed a burning path back up the soft skin of her throat until his lips lay over her thudding pulse where he let his fangs unsheathe. As her body began to contract around his fingers, Ian sank his fangs into her flesh and drank his fill, the warmth of her blood flowing over his tongue and into his mouth, filling him, satiating his gnawing hunger, fueling his unfulfilled desire.

Mona screamed as her orgasm rolled through her, clutching his shoulders tight, arching into him as if she couldn't get close enough. Ian kept the pace with his hand until she was totally fulfilled. After he licked the wounds on her neck closed, he found her slumberous emerald green gaze staring back at him, full of awe mixed with sensual mischief. He grinned, swiftly removed his clothes, and pulled her over to the bed.

Mona pushed him back against the headboard and settled beside him, curling her legs underneath her. When she stroked his cock with her hand, Ian rocked his hips, waiting in anticipation for her hot mouth to surround him. The warmth of her tongue, tracing a moist path around his hard erection, felt so good. He groaned his approval. Ian closed his eyes and bucked against her while he ran his hand up her spine to cup the back of her neck.

Sliding his hands into her hair, he directed her pace until she found the rhythm that had his balls tightening against him, his blood pumping faster in his body. Ian slowed his own impending climax down in order to take care of Mona's needs. There's no reason she shouldn't enjoy all the benefits a vampire could offer her.

He mentally ran his hands across her backside, skimming them closer to her swollen labia. Mona paused her movements, stilling against him. He knew the sensations surprised her because his hands were still in her hair. He whispered soothing words in her mind, assuring her. When she moaned against him, accepting what he offered her, Ian swiped an invisible finger across her clitoris and smiled at her sigh of contentment.

As he mentally slid two fingers inside her, she gave a delighted whimper and then moaned against his erection, spreading her legs and elevating her rear, silently asking for more. Ian accommodated her, adding a thumb to the mixture, rubbing it across her nub. Mona's mouth closed tighter around his cock as she rocked with his mental stimulation. Ian regretted he wasn't privy to her emotions. He needed to feel a much deeper connection with her to be able to experience her feelings, which was a shame, for he would dearly love to send all those sensations straight to Duncan.

When her increased pace on his shaft sent his need nearly spiraling out of control, Ian experienced the knotting pressure deep in his groin as he held back in order to send his own mental and physical sensations to his brother. He smirked in satisfaction when he heard the music abruptly stop, followed by Duncan's hissing intake of breath.

Duncan's presence, aggressive, angry, and thoroughly aroused, forced his way past Ian's mental barriers, entering his mind. Ian felt his brother's coiled anger, his resentment over Ian's sharing his feelings with him, his self-loathing that he couldn't resist the lure his twin passed on to him.

Duncan's words, full of sarcasm, entered his mind, *Ever felt another's orgasm, Ian?*

Before Ian could reply, Duncan turned the tables on him and forced him to accept Mona's thoughts and feelings, sending them to Ian in rapid, relentless succession—lust, passion, raging desire, tension, voices and chants, pleading and begging, internal thoughts and moans mixed with sensation after sensation slammed into his consciousness. Ian groaned and jerked at the sensory overload, coming so hard and so fast he thought his heart would burst from his chest.

When Mona finished with him, she pulled away as her own body trembled from the after effects of her orgasm. After she stopped shaking she looked up at him, her eyes wide, and said, "That was amazing."

Ian chuckled, pulled her into his arms, and kissed her. She sighed and snuggled against his chest. He held her close for a while before he ran a hand down her cheek and compelled her to sleep. He'd taken her blood and he knew she needed to rest.

He was pleased that he had gotten Duncan to participate, because Ian knew for Duncan to share Mona's thoughts and emotions with him, his brother would have to had experienced them himself.

Once he was dressed, Ian walked back downstairs to see Duncan sitting on the couch, staring into the fire. Ian grinned when he walked around the sofa to face his brother.

Duncan refused to look at him as he spoke, his face taut with anger, "I know you had the best intentions, Ian, but you need to stop trying to make me into someone I'm not."

Ian stretched and smiled as he sat down on the other end of the couch. He didn't let his brother's fierce expression bother him in the least. "I know you better than anyone, Duncan. You thoroughly enjoyed that. Admit it?"

Duncan's gaze lifted to the staircase. Ian knew his brother pictured Mona's beautiful body, her lush breasts and pink nipples jutting toward him, laid back across his burgundy silk comforter. When Ian saw the look of longing in his twin's face before he masked it behind an inscrutable expression, he vowed to himself he'd do everything in his power to help Duncan find happiness.

* * * * *

When the evening arrived, Lucian awoke quickly, having slept very little. The darkness couldn't come soon enough as far as his peace of mind was concerned. He had to know. Was Rana Sterling Elizabeth reborn?

As soon as he got up from bed, he immediately called the funeral home. The curator didn't have any recourse against his hypnotic voice. He gave Lucian the information he sought. Armed with Rana's address, Lucian shapeshifted into a raven in mere seconds and took off toward his destiny.

Without a sound, he folded his raven's wings and landed on her balcony. Shifting into mist, he slid between the French doors and materialized near her bed.

She stirred and turned toward him. Even though he could see her features perfectly with his night vision, he moved so the moonlight shined on her face, its gentle glow accentuating her rosy skin.

He recognized the heart-shaped face with high cheekbones and a strong chin as the woman he'd seen a week ago—the woman who'd slammed him with intense physical awareness with only a brush of her shoulder.

He wanted to run his fingers through the ash-blond hair splayed across her pillow, touch her full lips, curved in sleep as if she were smiling at something or someone.

Her hand rested on the pillow near her cheek, the ring's stones catching the moon's bright light. Lucian reached out and touched his creation. The ring, made of a special amalgam he'd had created by a gypsy metallurgist, was meant to absorb its wearer's scent. His heart pounded, blood rushed to fill his erection, making him more aware of his naked state. He'd been so enthralled with seeing Rana again, he hadn't thought to create the illusion of clothes once he'd shifted to human form.

He sank to his knees beside the bed, gently lifted her hand and brought it to his nose, inhaling. Peace washed over him. After seventy years of waiting, he'd finally found her. The scent was his, mixed with hers — different than he remembered Elizabeth's to be, because now the ring carried Rana's own special smell — sweet, with a hint of citrus.

This woman's alluring fragrance magnified tenfold the response he'd had to Elizabeth. He hadn't anticipated how keenly it would affect him. The fire in his veins burned intensely. Lucian closed his eyes, thankful for a second chance.

Looking at her face once more, so beautiful and peaceful in sleep, his chest contracted with love; he heard her heart beating, the rush of her warm blood coursing through her veins.

He imagined her writhing under him, arching her back, baring her neck. "Make love to me, Lucian," she'd call out frantically. The fantasy brought a smile to his lips. He touched her hair and whispered, "Soon, my love. Soon." He turned, shimmered into mist and left the way he came.

* * * * *

Rana awoke to the blaring beep of her alarm clock. She moaned and hit the snooze button with her palm. Nine minutes later, the offending noise sounded again.

She grimaced and pulled herself out of bed, looking longingly at her novel that had fallen to the floor last night.

She'd never been much of a morning person, always preferring to stay up late, reading into the wee hours of the morning. Splaying her fingers against her scalp, she combed through her tangled mass of hair and stared bleary-eyed at herself in the mirror. "Ugh! I need a shower," she mumbled as she drew her hands over her face.

The scent of lavender, strong and sweet tickled her nostrils. Rana tilted her hand and sniffed the ring on her finger. The odor was strong and clean and now included a citrus smell as well. It was definitely coming from the ring. Odd, that. How long can a ring carry the prior owner's scent? Hmmm, she really liked the perfume. Maybe she'd head down to the department store at lunch and see if they recognized the flowery aroma.

Fearful of washing the scent away, she reached up to remove the ring from her finger and found it lodged in place. No matter how hard she tugged, it wouldn't budge. Finally, she gave up, oddly comforted by the fact the ring seemed to have become a part of her. She just hoped her bath wouldn't dilute the fragrance too much.

* * * * *

Rana parked her car, waited on the curb for rush hour traffic, paused, and then walked across the street to open her bookstore. She lifted the ring to her nose and smiled, pleased her shower hadn't erased the pleasant scent.

Inside, she snapped the shades up and turned the Closed sign to Open before shutting the door behind her.

The bookstore's heavy aroma of old and new books greeted her like an old friend. There was nothing she enjoyed more. Well, except for the smell of her new ring. Her smile broadened at the thought.

She'd set up the shop with more than just browsing in mind, adding an elevated area right next to the big picture window to be used as a reading corner. A carpeted floor scattered with brightly colored oversized pillows and cushioned chairs waited for readers to enjoy a good book. Twice a month, she had cookies and drinks for her customers, encouraging them to sit down and read while in her store.

The bell above the door chimed, bringing her out of her reverie. She turned as David walked in, carrying a potted plant with a red bow.

"Good morning, David. Enjoying your fall break?"

He nodded and handed her the plant. "I'm sorry about your grandfather, Rana."

Tears stung her eyes. No, not here. She wasn't going to cry. She needed to be strong. Rana gave David a tremulous smile and took the plant from him. "Thank you for thinking of me."

The silence stretched out between them and David shifted uncomfortably from one foot to the next as if he didn't know what to say next.

With an inward smile, Rana decided to put the poor guy out of his misery. "Jack left me his 'Vette."

David's eyes lit up. "Really? Your grandfather was so cool, Rana."

She laughed. "I know. Have you come to see the new books?"

"Got any on werewolves?" he asked eagerly.

Rana shook her head. "Well, not any new books."

At David's forlorn expression, she pointed to two boxes in front of the counter. "I just bought a slew of used books. You could go through them and see if there's anything in there."

David's eyes lit up. "Awesome. I'll help you catalogue them, okay?"

Rana laughed. "Sure, and whatever you find on werewolves you can keep as long as your parents say it's okay."

David grinned and began opening the boxes.

They worked in companionable silence as they pulled out, tagged and cataloged the books for the used bookshelf.

"Ah, ha." She lifted a book and swung it underneath his nose, a grin on her face. "What about a book on vampires?"

David's expression showed no interest. "No thanks. I only want ones on werewolves."

Rana chuckled and continued with her work.

As lunchtime approached, David rose and stretched. "I'll be back in an hour, okay Rana?"

Rana smiled at his all-business tone. "I'll see you then."

When David left, she locked up her store and walked the three blocks down to Bennett's department store.

Approaching the perfume counter, she said, "Hi, I'm trying to find a particular scent."

"Sure." The bubbly blond behind the counter smiled. "What's the name?"

Rana gave her an apologetic smile. "I don't know."

She tried to pull off the ring once more, but the darn thing may as well have been welded to her finger. Finally, she lifted her hand, her cheeks flushed in embarrassment and said, "Well, it smells like this ring."

Candice, or so her nametag read, leaned forward and sniffed the ring. Leaning back, she said in a polite voice, "I don't smell anything."

Rana frowned and smelled the ring once more. As strong as can be, the ring radiated a citrus-lavender fragrance.

"What does it smell like to you?" Candice offered.

Rana looked at her and said absently, "Oh, the closest I could get to defining the scent would be lavender with a hint of citrus."

Candice bent over and pulled out two bottles of perfume. "This one has lavender and this one has lemons and oranges. We don't have any that has both." She grinned. "Though it does sound like an intriguing combination."

Rana picked up one and then the other, but neither smelled at all like her ring. She smiled. "Thanks, I think I'll keep looking."

She walked out of the store, surprised that the girl behind the counter couldn't differentiate the scent. Maybe being surrounded by all those fragrances dulled her sense of smell. She lifted the ring to her nose once more. The metal still smelled like lavender but now the citrus smell seemed more pronounced. Weird. Well, if the ring continued to emit this scent, she wouldn't need any perfume anyway.

She made it back to her store and spent the rest of the afternoon showing new books to visiting customers.

While she rang up a customer, David let out a hoot of excitement and jumped up from the floor. "I've got one."

"Found a book on werewolves?" Rana smiled at his excitement.

David grinned. "Can I take it home and read it after I finish these last couple of books?"

Rana waved her hand. "Go on now. It's almost time to go home anyway."

The customer, an older lady, smiled and followed David out of the store.

Rana glanced at her watch. *Ten more minutes and it's quittin' time,* she thought to herself.

She bent over and picked up the last two books. The bell chimed and a man walked in. Rana glanced up and saw him browsing through a shelf of autobiographies.

She did a double-take and inspected him closer while his gaze was averted. Short-cropped midnight hair, and high cheekbones flowed into a straight nose. Her stomach tightened in response to his sensual mouth and strong jaw line.

His black trench coat hid his build, though its length only accentuated his height, which she guessed to be about six-three. The cut of his white dress shirt and charcoal gray slacks screamed custom made. What was he doing in her small bookstore? He had the look of a Barrett's shopper.

She quickly glanced down at her chocolate brown sweater and long black skirt. *Note to self: your clothes suck! Update them and for the love of Jimmy, get some color girl.* She lifted her head with a wry smile and asked, "Can I help you with something?"

He turned and white teeth gleamed in a charming grin. "Hi," he called out. "I'm just looking."

Her heart flopped in her chest at that devastating smile and then did a somersault when she met his metallic gaze and realized he was the man from the cemetery.

Rana worked hard to keep her voice steady. "Take your time."

She put one book on the shelf and noticed the other hadn't been tagged. Behind the counter, she attached a tag and returned to the used bookshelf.

The man stood in front of the tall wooden case, inspecting the titles, a thoughtful look on his face. "How old are some of these books? The titles seem to go back a few decades."

His pale gray eyes met hers and her heart tripped a beat. She let out a nervous, throaty laugh. "Yes, some of the books on the left date back as early as 1930."

The curve of that sensual mouth and the warmth of his smile, took her breath away. "I'm a collector of sorts."

The man absolutely mesmerized her. His speech was formal and cultured, more...old school. She found the cadence in the deep timbre of his voice extremely sexy, almost hypnotic. Shaking her head to clear it, she finally remembered to speak. "Well, browse to your heart's content." She lifted the book to shelve it when long, warm fingers encircled her wrist, catching her hand in midair.

Rana sucked in her breath at the electric contact and turned questioning eyes his way. For some inexplicable reason, she wasn't afraid of him, only intensely aware of how much he affected her.

"Did you just get this one in? What's it about?" He indicated the book in her hand.

"It's a book about vampires." She laughed. "I doubt it's your kind of reading."

45

He raised a dark eyebrow, amusement obvious as his hand remained clasped around her wrist. "What kind of books do I look like I would read?" As he awaited her answer, he rubbed his thumb over her pounding pulse, causing liquid fire to course throughout her body, settling between her legs in throbbing heat. She became immensely aware of his nearness, his clean masculine scent.

Rana pulled her arm from his grasp, opened the book, and read an excerpt, "'They are the undead, forever doomed to walk the night in search of their next meal. The beating pulse of their victim calls to their basest instinct: to feed.'"

She glanced up to meet his gaze and grinned, but his eyes were on her throat, his expression intrigued. As if he sensed her stare, he raised his silver gaze to hers and a slow, sexy smile formed on his lips. "Now why does that sound so sensual when you read it versus how I'm sure it's intended to be taken?"

Rana blushed, feeling the heat infuse her cheeks, and swiftly turned to put the book on the shelf, glancing over her shoulder to answer him. "My guess is your taste runs more in the non-fiction section."

"You mean you don't believe in vampires?"

Enough flirting, Rana girl, she reminded herself. "Certainly not." She had to stand on her tiptoes to place the book on the right shelf. Her foot slipped and her wrist grazed the wooden shelf, catching on its rough edge as she grabbed a lower one for support. "Ow!" *Damn that hurt.* She had to clench her jaw to keep from repeating the explicative that came to mind.

The man's arms went around her waist, righting her.

"Are you okay?"

Rana tensed at the sensation of his strong arms around her—the rightness. She brushed his hands away. "Yes, I'm fine. Just a little clumsy tonight."

She started to walk away when he caught her arm once more, his dark brows drawing together. "You're hurt."

She looked down at his coat sleeve. Though black she could see where drops of moisture stood out on the smooth material.

Beads of blood surfaced in the long, red gash on her wrist. That's going to look lovely tomorrow, she thought wryly. "Oh, I'm sorry about your coat."

Holding her arm, he gently rubbed his thumb over her wound, erasing the blood, but it just resurfaced again. When his eyes met hers, his nostrils flared and he held her gaze for a long, tense moment before he spoke. "Do you have some antiseptic to clean your wound?"

Rana nodded mutely and walked behind the counter to open the first aid kit.

Without a word, he took the alcohol swab from her, and rubbed it tenderly over the cut. The alcohol stung and she winced reflexively. She stared at him, wondering why in the world she let this complete stranger take care of her.

He leaned over and blew on her wound, looking up at her with a mischievous smile. "It always helped when I was a kid. Do you have any band aids?"

While he held her arm, she turned to retrieve a band-aid and felt his finger rub across her wound once more. She quickly turned back to see him holding out his hand with an expectant look on his face.

"Blood was surfacing again," he explained.

She placed the band-aid in his hand and he put the bandage on her arm with precise, measured movements, making her feel cherished and protected. *Now why would I think such a silly, fanciful thing?* Rana handed him a wipe, careful to keep her expression neutral. "Here, so you can clean the blood off your hand."

He waved it away with a smile. "No need. I took care of it."

"Oh," she said, wondering what he'd cleaned his hand with. "I'll gladly pay to have your coat dry cleaned," she offered.

He smiled, his gaze locking with hers as he rubbed his thumb along the fleshy part of her hand. "Come have dinner with me instead." The words reverberated in an echoing whisper over and over in her mind like a sing-song chant.

Surprised by his dinner invitation, she drew her hand away, briskly collected the trash and put the first aid kit back together, snapping the lid closed. With a polite smile, she shook her head. "I don't even know you." When all she really wanted to do was say, "Yes," to a total stranger. Was she nuts?

"But we've already met once," he said with a sexy smile.

She sucked in her breath. "You remember me from the cemetery?" Whom had he been there to see? Had he suffered a loss just as she had?

His expression turned tender. "How could I forget you? You looked very sad that day. I'm sorry for your loss."

His mention of Jack's death reminded her how emotionally fragile she was. She didn't need a relationship right now, even if she felt a strong connection with this man. She shook off the feeling of familiarity. He was still a stranger.

"I don't think so."

Tsk, tsk, using me as an excuse. She heard Jack's voice in her head as if he were leaning over her shoulder.

Oh, shut up, Jack. I'm trying to respect the dead.

Yeah, right.

She raised her eyebrow. "Are you done shopping? I'm about to close up for the night."

He nodded and headed for the door; his movements fluid and graceful as if he didn't really walk, but glided across the floor. He opened the door and met her gaze. "Yes, I found what I was looking for. Good night."

"Good night," she called after him, not sure what to make of the man. He'd said he'd found what he was looking for, but he didn't buy a thing.

Chapter Four

Lucian stood outside *The Lion's Lair*, waiting for Kraid to exit. He'd seen the vamp seducing two young women on the dance floor. Although he knew it wouldn't be long before Kraid led the women outside, frustration mounted as leaned against the wall. Maybe it was best he couldn't find Kraid last night after he'd fed. Now he'd had two days to build his strength. Tonight was about setting the vamp straight, but he'd fight him if it came to that.

Kraid exited the club, nuzzling the neck of one of the blondes. Her twin, flanking his other side, ran her long red nails down his chest.

Lucian stepped out of the shadows, blocking his path.

"Kraid. We need to talk."

Kraid looked up at him and laughed dismissively. "Later."

"No. Now, Kraid." Lucian didn't move. He looked at the women and compelled them. "You're tired and you want to go home."

"No." Kraid tightened his grip on her waist.

One woman speared her fingers through his short, spiky brown hair, saying, "I'm really tired, Kraid. I'll see you later, okay?" She turned and walked off toward her car. The other kissed his cheek and followed her sister, blowing him a goodbye kiss.

Kraid started to follow her, but Lucian put his hand on his chest. "I said now."

"What do you want?" Kraid snapped, narrowing his green eyes at him.

"I want you to keep your clan in line, Kraid. I heard about the killings." He fixed his long-time rival with a steely stare. "That's unacceptable."

Kraid elevated his chin. "Who are you to tell me what's acceptable or not?"

"I'm accepting the Vité position." Lucian gave him a lazy, confident smile. "So you see, I have every right."

He noted the surprise in Kraid's eyes and the pure hatred that followed before the vamp masked it with an insolent smile.

"The vote has to be unanimous, Lucian. And I won't vote for you."

Lucian ignored his comment. "I'm here to talk about the humans who were killed, Kraid."

Kraid buffed his nails on the lapel of his jacket and affected a bored expression. "The human I killed was a vampire hunter. He deserved to die." He lifted his shoulders in a nonchalant shrug. "I'm not sure about the other two."

Lucian clenched his jaw at the man's complete lack of responsibility. "You'll answer to the council for your actions. Punish the other offenders in your clan or I will."

"Why are you acting like I've committed some crime?" Kraid gritted his teeth in anger. "The man was a vampire hunter."

"Because you're the leader of your clan and are responsible for the Bruens' actions."

"I don't see what the big deal is."

Lucian took a step closer and leaned toward Kraid

with menace. "You and your clan's stupidity puts us all in danger." He flung his arm out toward the open parking lot, his anger rising. "There are vampire hunters out there who would love to rid this world of all vamps, and they're just waiting for us to screw up. We're the minority. We must learn to live among humans as best we can." He saved the best for last as he pinned Kraid with a meaningful stare. "If you can't curb your clan, Ian will take your place."

The veins bulging on Kraid's temple displayed how hard he worked to control his temper. Finally, he snorted and cocked his head to the side. "So, why the sudden interest in the Vité position, Lucian, hmmm?"

Before he could respond, Kraid's eyes lit up with delightful glee. "Don't tell me you've found your 'mate'?" He laughed heartily as he had done for many years at what he considered Lucian's softness.

Lucian kept his expression carefully dispassionate.

Kraid inhaled deeply. "I smell her weak human's blood on you." He flared his nostrils and slid his tongue across his teeth. "And the scent is pure, untainted by another vamp." He smiled, showing his fangs. "Maybe I'll have a go at her."

Blind red rage encompassed Lucian. He grabbed Kraid by the neck and slammed him up against the wall, baring his fangs with a hiss. "If you go anywhere near her, I'll rip your heart out with my bare hands."

Lucian ignored Kraid's attempts to loosen his hand and tightened it around his windpipe. Even though vamps only took a few breaths per minute, he only had to hold him long enough to cut off his air. His entire body tense and coiled with fury, Lucian said in a deadly voice, "Am I making myself clear?"

Kraid managed a strangled affirmative noise. He let him drop to the ground. While Kraid gasped for breath, Lucian finished, "Get your clan in order. You have to answer to the council in three days."

He turned to walk away, but Kraid couldn't help one last taunt. "Why would you even consider diluting the Kantrue blood with an insignificant human?"

Lucian didn't dignify his question with an answer. He opened the nightclub's door and walked inside.

* * * * *

Rana lay on the bed, naked, her eyes closed, her body heat igniting to a slow, steady burn, her sex throbbing in anticipation. He leaned over her and kissed her neck before sliding his lips down to her breast. Grasping a taut nipple in his hot, moist mouth, he took a long, hard drag.

She gasped and arched her back toward him, clutching his broad, muscular shoulders, reveling in the powerful tendons flexing underneath her fingers and the surge of lust that shot through her body.

He kissed a path to her other breast and lavished it with equal attention while his hand traced her stomach muscles and lower until he touched her damp curls.

She moaned in pleasure when his finger slid inside. "Open for me, Rana," he whispered in her ear.

His intimate words fueled her desire, making her ache for him. She opened her legs wider, wanting, needing his touch. He added another finger and plunged them both deep into her before he drew them back out, spreading her moist warmth around her, playing with her clitoris.

"You're so wet and utterly responsive." Satisfaction laced

his desire-filled tone.

Passion built and she panted as sweet, thrumming tension coiled within her.

He lifted his head and his pale gray eyes met hers. Rana's heart jerked when she immediately recognized the man from her store.

The shock of making love to a complete stranger jolted her out of her seductive, erotic dream. She sat up in bed, breathing hard, her heart pounding as she clutched the covers around her.

Sensing a presence, she turned toward the French doors and sucked in a breath when she saw a man's outline in the night shadows. Somehow she knew it was the man from her dream.

"I must still be dreaming. I've conjured you up in my mind," she whispered.

He took a step forward and the moonlight reflected on his face. "Don't be afraid. I won't hurt you."

She smiled. "I'm not afraid. What's your name?"

"My name is Lucian." His smile was tender. "And yours is Rana. I like the way your name sounds on my lips."

She did too. To her foggy, sleep-filled brain it sounded like an endearment.

His gaze raked her naked shoulders and arms, lingering on the spaghetti straps of her nightgown. The fire in his eyes turned hot and intense. "Will you invite me in, dear Rana?"

The fierceness of his gaze made her completely aware of her half-dressed state. Rana pulled the covers closer. She might not be afraid of him but he was still a stranger. "No."

He sighed, his expression disappointed. "Then go back to sleep, love."

She shook her head. "Not while you're here."

He grinned. "Your wish is my command. Sweet dreams, my Rana." He shimmered and disappeared.

Rana rubbed her eyes and blinked at the spot Lucian had stood. She lay back on her bed and closed her eyes, her heart beating against her ribcage. Man, that was some dream, a very vivid dream. Goosebumps formed on her arms when she realized the ache between her legs was very real, very real indeed. She tossed and turned until exhaustion finally took over.

* * * * *

Lucian reappeared as soon as she fell back to sleep. He stood beside her bed and stared adoringly at her, reliving their shared passion. His shaft throbbed, begging for release, but he tamped down the unfulfilled ache. He welcomed the discomfort. It felt good to be alive again after feeling dead for so long. He wanted to be near her. He *needed* to be near her. He needed the closeness so much he was breaking a cardinal vampire rule: a vampire must be given permission to enter another's home.

During the day, he'd woo her as any man would court his mate, but at night she was all his to love and bring to heights of passion. He'd only satisfy her, however, not himself. She'd have to ask him to stay before he allowed himself that pleasure. He'd risk the insanity until she succumbed.

And she would. He closed his eyes and drew in his breath, inhaling her aroused feminine scent, reveling in the heat emanating from her soft skin. Lucian willed himself to remain calm as he reached out an unsteady hand to touch the cascade of hair on her pillow.

Her gorgeous shoulder-length hair pleased him immensely. And her hazel green eyes, filled with sadness at first but quick to humor, drew him in. Her coloring was nothing like Elizabeth's, but the soul, the intensity, the connection was there, even stronger than before.

His entire body shook with his desire to taste her. Earlier, when she'd hurt herself, an overwhelming need to protect rushed through him. He'd done what he could to help her heal, but rubbing his healing saliva on her arm only made him want her more. The sight of her bright red blood stoked the fire burning inside him to pure unadulterated lust.

The taste of those tiny droplets he'd swept from her arm only managed to whet his appetite. He'd relished the flavor, sweet and pure, a decidedly erotic combination especially considering the passionate side of her he'd seen tonight. He might be tortured, but he could wait. Their joining would be that much sweeter for it in the end.

* * * * *

Rana spent the entire next day thinking of the man named Lucian. Well, at least in her dream his name was Lucian. She smiled that her subconscious had created such a dangerous sounding name for him. But then—she blushed when she remembered her dream's passionate nature—danger seemed to fit right in with the theme. Where had this wanton nature been all her life? Oh, she'd had a couple of boyfriends in the past, but no one affected her the way the man in her dream had. The thought both disturbed and thrilled her at the same time.

She'd even chosen her outfit with him in mind. Her hunter green, fine gauge sweater clung to her upper body, displaying her curves, which weren't near enough, she thought with a wry smile. She'd coupled the sweater with a patterned wool skirt that stopped a few inches above her knees. Soft leather knee high boots completed her outfit.

As if her thoughts had conjured him up, the man from yesterday walked into her store, holding the door open for a customer to leave. This afternoon he wore a navy v-neck sweater and faded jeans. And those jeans fit his toned physique all too well, she noted as her body quickened in response. When he smiled at her, her heart jerked at the physical pull she felt toward him.

A customer walked up and asked her a question about a historical novel, drawing her attention away. Before she walked off to help the lady find the book she sought, Rana met his gaze once more and smiled back.

As she rang up the customer's novel, she noted the man from her dream had settled into a chair in the reading corner. He was immersed in one of the leather hardbound collector's edition books. Which one caught his attention? she wondered.

She didn't have time to contemplate him further as several women walked in with their children in tow. Rana smiled, knowing she'd just received a whole slew of children's books. The children immediately ran over to the reading corner, picked books out of the wicker basket on the floor, and sprawled out on the carpeted area to flip through them.

"Would you like to see the new books we just got in?" Rana asked the mothers.

"Yes," they replied in unison and Rana showed them

the bookshelf where the new books resided.

While the women browsed through the books, Rana noted her male visitor still had his head bent over his book. She picked up a basket full of books and walked over to another bookcase. Bending to collect several books, she stood and slid them onto the shelf. Rana backed up, placed her hands on her hips, and bit her bottom lip as she decided how she wanted to display the books.

Larger than a standard sized book, the map books warranted a shelf on their own, but she didn't want to put them up so high readers couldn't see them. Sighing at her dilemma, she flipped her hair over her shoulder and involuntarily shivered when she felt something brush against her bared neck as if someone stood behind her and softly ran a hand across her skin.

She looked up and her eyes locked with the man's silver ones. He leaned back in the chair, his book lying in his lap, and stared at her intently. Seemingly calm and unruffled by the children chattering around him, his gaze skimmed over her body in a slow, sensual sweep before his eyes met hers once more. Unmistakable desire flickered in those striking pale pools before he smiled and picked up his book once more. Her stomach clenched and a thrill shot through her at the thought of this dynamic man seeming to want her.

When he opened the book and broke their gaze, an idea suddenly popped into her head: top shelf, because the kids will get to them otherwise. A sign at eye level pointing to the map books should do the trick. Spurred into action by her out-of-nowhere brainstorm, Rana moved behind the counter to make the sign.

While she taped the sign up on the wall, the sound of the man's deep voice caused Rana to pause her movements. She looked up to see him reading one of the storybooks to the children. They all sat around him, their faces raised in rapt attention. As he told the age-old story of Little Red Riding Hood, she found herself jumping when he described the wolf pouncing out of bed after little Red Riding Hood. There was something about his voice, the steady, self-assured intonation with which he spoke which mesmerized all who listened. Rana shook her head with a smile. He was like the Pied Piper, leading them along on a merry adventure.

When he finished the story, she heard clapping behind her and realized that the mothers had also stopped their browsing to listen to him tell the story. He looked up at the clapping and grinned sheepishly. Rana smiled her approval, openly laughing when the children demanded more.

The last hour few by and when the last customer left, Rana stood behind the counter, unable to move as he put the book he'd been reading back and approached. She knew she must look like a deer caught in headlights. She'd been comfortable with his attention when there were people around, but now that they were alone, her heart rammed so hard in her chest, it was a wonder he didn't hear it.

Forcing an unaffected smile, she asked, "Did you enjoy your book?" She'd finally discovered he'd been reading the book on Turn of the Century Inventions.

He smiled back. "Yes. How's your arm?"

"Healing quite nicely, actually." That was an understatement. When she looked at the wound this morning and saw it was almost completely healed, she'd been totally surprised.

She met his penetrating gaze and wondered what he would think if he knew he'd played a starring role in her fantasy dream the night before. The secret brought a playful smile to her lips.

He leaned forward, a curious expression on his face. "Care to share?"

Her cheeks grew hot under his close scrutiny. She cleared her throat, thrusting aside all thoughts about last night.

Go on, Rana. Give the man a fantasy to hold onto.

Go away, Jack.

"Um, no." She lifted a stack of books from the counter and walked across the shop, passing him on the way to the shelves. "So, if you're not buying the book on inventions, are you back to buy that vampire book?" She teased without turning.

"No." His chest touched her back as he breathed the word in her ear. She dropped the books with a cry. How'd he move so quickly behind her?

Rana bent to retrieve the books. He squatted beside her and handed her a hardcover mystery. "You scared me," she accused, meeting his steady gaze.

A look of guilt passed over his face. "Sorry, I didn't mean to frighten you."

"It's okay." She couldn't help but smile at his contrite expression. Standing, she lifted the books.

He stood as well and shoved his hands in his front pockets, a devilish grin riding up his face. "I hope you'll accept my dinner invitation tonight."

Focusing on the books as she put them on the shelf, she contemplated him. She knew nothing about the man accept he was incredibly attractive. This probably wasn't a good idea.

He moved closer until his chest touched her arm. "Come on, go out with me. Let me get to know you."

"I don't even know your name." She chuckled and faced him, taking a step back.

He looked pleased as he answered her, "My name is Lucian Trevane."

Blood rushed to her head at his words. The floor pitched beneath her. He reached out and grabbed her upper arms. "Are you okay?"

Rana shook her head to clear it. Okay, this just wigged her out that she'd guessed his name. *Jack, did you put the mojo on me when you died and pass along your psychic abilities? A warning would've been nice.*

She backed away from his touch. "No, I'm fine." Putting out her hand, she said, "My name's Rana Sterling."

He took her hand and instead of shaking it, he kissed the back of her fingers, his silver eyes locked with hers. "It's nice to meet you, Rana."

Tiny shock waves rolled down her arm and into her chest. Her breasts tingled, heavy with desire.

Before she could pull her hand away, he inhaled deeply. "I love your scent. It reminds me of citrus and honeysuckle."

Another shock. Talk about your electrical responses. If he keeps this up she just might go into cardiac arrest. Wouldn't that be great—dropping dead at the man's feet? Hey, at least she'd give him a shock for a change. "You can smell it?" Well, he obviously smelled something, but he'd gotten it all wrong.

She lifted the ring to her nose and said, "No, it's lavend—" But she stopped speaking when she realized he was right. She smelled citrus and honeysuckle. Okay, lovely, she'd just spent four hundred dollars on a revolving scent ring—a mood ring would be easier to explain. This was just plain weird. Well, at least he confirmed she wasn't going completely nuts, and so far she liked the various fragrance combinations.

She looked up at him and smiled. "You're right."

"Of course." He grinned. "It's intoxicating."

His nearness, his heat reached out and penetrated her clothes, seeping into her skin. Before she knew it, she said, "I'll go to dinner with you." Now why did she just agree to go to dinner with him? Oh yeah, that moth to the flame thing. Don't the stupid moths know it's really a bug zapper?

At his triumphant smile, she put up her hand. "But I'll meet you at the restaurant."

He nodded and they made arrangements to meet at the *China Jade* restaurant downtown.

* * * * *

"Hi." Rana slid into the chair across from him and thanked the waiter for her menu.

"Hey." He grinned.

After she'd placed her order, Rana turned to him, curiosity getting the best of her. "What were you really looking for when you came into my store the other night?"

"I was looking for something I'd lost a long time ago." His gray eyes twinkled.

Remembering he said he'd found what he was

looking for, her eyes lit up. "Really? Why haven't you bought the book then?"

Lucian smiled and put his hand over hers. "Rana, I've looked a long time for you."

She swallowed hard. That sounded way too specific. "Um, don't you mean someone like me?"

He slowly shook his head. "No, I mean you. I've searched all my life and I finally found you."

Stalker? No, obsessive. No, weird. No, possessive. Yes, possessive described the look in his eyes. Oh, boy, and she was really starting to like him, too, darn it! So why did that look make her feel so wanted? She never did make good decisions when she wasn't her normal self. And losing Jack would certainly qualify.

Rana pulled her hand away and looked at her watch. "You know, I just remembered I have something I need to take care of…"

"Rana."

She rambled on, "Yeah, I promised my parents I'd…"

"Rana." If his calm tone didn't stop her babbling, his warm hand covering hers once more certainly did.

"Hmmm?" She met his gaze warily.

He smiled a slow tilting of the lips that was oh, so sexy. "Do you believe in Kismet?"

"As in fate?"

He nodded slowly while his thumb traced circles inside her palm.

"My grandfather did."

"And did you trust your grandfather's opinion?"

She gave a wry smile. "Most of the time."

His silver gaze held hers. "Then trust that I mean you no harm. I only want to get to know you." *Trust me. Trust me.* His words made a whispering echo in her head. Man, how'd he do that?

His expression was so sincere. For some reason she couldn't fathom, she did trust him, explicitly. Regret washed over her. Pulling her hand from his, she said, "I'm sorry, but I can't give you what you're looking for."

He smiled, his eyes tender. "What's wrong? I see sadness in your eyes."

Tears welled up at his genuine interest in her well-being. "I recently lost my grandfather. That's the funeral I was attending when you saw me."

She rubbed her throbbing temples, disappointment in herself overwhelming her. "I'm in no shape to get involved with anyone." Tears threatened to fall.

He captured her hand once more, lacing his fingers with hers. "Give me a chance to get to know you, Rana. That's all I ask."

She sniffed back her tears and gave him a trembling smile. "I don't know what to say."

The deep timbre in his low laugh went straight to her toes. "Say you'll come dancing with me tomorrow night."

He wasn't looking for more than she could give. He just wanted to dance. That's not so bad. Dancing was a safe, no strings attached type of date. She nodded with a smile. "Yes, I'll go dancing with you." She cocked her head to the side. "What about you? Why were you at the cemetery?"

"I was saying goodbye to someone I knew a long time ago."

He didn't elaborate so they moved on to discussing a

varied range of subjects while they ate. She learned Lucian also collected books and from his descriptions his collection rivaled her private one.

"Do you have any siblings?" he asked.

She shook her head. "What about you?"

"Yes, I have a sister, Sabryn." He chuckled. "She's quite a pistol."

Rana's brows drew together as she worked the chopsticks, picking up a piece of chicken. "Sabryn, that's an unusual name. I recently met a woman named Sabryn."

He raised a curious eyebrow. "Oh, really?"

She nodded, set down the chopsticks and lifted her left hand. "I bought this ring from her a couple of days ago."

He clasped her hand in his warm one and inspected the ring. "Unusual design."

"I thought so, too. And for some reason, once I put it on, I didn't want to take it off." She laughed. "And now, I couldn't blast the darn thing off my finger if my life depended on it."

He chuckled at her words while he ran his thumb over the ring, sliding his finger down to caress her skin. "I like it. The ring suits you."

Dinner was over way too soon and after Lucian had taken care of the bill, he walked her outside. His brow rose as they approached the electric blue sports car.

She laughed and answered his unspoken question. "It was my grandfather's. He was much more flamboyant than me."

He clasped her hand. "I think it fits your personality well."

She gave him an are-you-nuts look. "Yeah, right. That's me, wild Rana."

He smiled. "You're a very passionate woman, Rana. One I want to get to know better."

The crisp fall wind whipped around them, making her shiver. Lucian pulled the lapels of her coat closer together. His caring, thoughtful gesture melted her heart. She smiled up at him. He ran his thumb slowly along her jaw line as if memorizing the contours of her face and lifted her hand to his nose, inhaling her scent.

"May I kiss you?"

Yes, she wanted to scream. *If you don't, I'll kiss you.* She nodded.

He smelled so good, like an exotic aroma she couldn't place. The description eluded her. The scent was like being in the woods after a fresh rain with a spicy fragrance wafting through the trees all around her.

He cupped her face in his big hands and murmured as his lips touched hers, "I have to know if you taste as good as you smell."

Threading his fingers through her hair, he pulled her closer. Rana grasped the elbows of his winter coat and opened her mouth under his persuasive lips. His warm tongue took one long sensuous stroke against hers before hungrily coming back for more. It was just like the kiss from her dream—intimate and thorough.

He tasted like the peppermints the waitress had handed them at the end of their meal, refreshing and cool, mixed with hot male desire—a stimulating combination. She returned his devouring kiss, needing the contact, reveling in it.

He pressed her against her car, his hips pinning her in

place. "You taste better than I could've ever imagined," he whispered hoarsely while he trailed his lips over her jaw.

Rana gave a soft sigh and let her head fall back, exposing her neck for his tantalizing kisses. When they didn't come, she opened her eyes and stared at him, worried she'd somehow done something wrong. His nostrils flared as he stared at the expanse of her neck, his entire body tensed against her.

She chuckled. "It's okay, Lucian, I don't bite."

He flashed a smile, his eyes meeting hers. "Oh, but I do, sweet Rana."

She stifled a giggle. "As long as you don't draw blood, I'm fine with love bites."

One hand on her hip, the other entangled in her hair, Lucian's eyes flamed with desire as he gently tugged the handful, tilting her head, exposing her throat.

"You have such a beautiful neck."

Her throaty laugh turned to a gasp of pleasure as he trailed blazing kisses down her neck and back up. His hot tongue laved her skin while his hold on her tightened and his hips gently ground against her, his rigid flesh unmistakable.

Liquid heat gathered between her thighs. The aching pressure became more than she could handle. She pressed back, a counter to his rhythmic thrusts. He growled low in his throat at her response, his teeth grazing her skin, causing goosebumps to form all over. She moaned in anticipation and dropped her hands to his lower back, pulling him closer.

Laughter penetrated her foggy brain and reality came rushing back. A group had exited the restaurant and was making their way to their cars. They joked amongst themselves. She tensed, and Lucian's grip on her tightened, his teeth clamped on her neck, pinning her still.

She whispered his name once and then more forcefully when he responded by pulling her closer and applying pressure. Finally, he lifted his head, his entire body tightly coiled, his expression totally focused. Shaking his head as if to clear his mind, he finally seemed to come back to the present.

He dropped his hands, stepped away, and gave her a half smile. "I'm sorry, Rana. You had me so caught up, I forgot where I was."

She laughed softly. "Well, that makes a girl feel good."

But Lucian's stepping away was a good thing, too. It cleared her brain so she didn't make a hormonally driven statement like, "Come home with me so we can finish what we started."

No, she liked Lucian. She wanted whatever was happening between them to take time, even if it was a slow, simmering burn. That way, she'd be sure the intense passion that they seemed to share was real and not because she'd be using him to fill the well of grief left by Jack's death.

Lucian grasped her hand and brought her hand to his mouth. His silver eyes searched hers as he placed a kiss on her palm. "Dance with me tomorrow night?"

Rana smiled. "Yes, let me give you directions to my house."

Lowering her hand, he laced his fingers with hers, shaking his head. "I'll find you." The warmth of his confident smile spread through her like the first rays of spring sunshine, taking her breath away.

Rana returned his smile, giddy with the knowledge he wanted to *find* her and not have the information so freely given. She withdrew her hand and opened her car door. "See you tomorrow night around seven-thirty?"

He nodded. "Good night, sweet Rana."

She climbed into her car and drove off, her thighs tingling, her sex throbbing in unfulfilled desire. What would it be like when he slid inside her? She squirmed in her seat, because in her heart she knew—it would be mind-blowing. Rana punched the gas and kicked the car into a higher gear, smiling at the rumble of the engine vibrating beneath her thighs. Oh, yeah, Jack definitely got his jollies!

Chapter Five

Lucian leaned over her, his lips barely touching hers. "I want to touch you."

The low timber of his voice, so utterly male, raised goosebumps on her flesh as Rana ran her hands over the powerfully built surface of his naked chest and arms. His skin felt warm and hard, his muscles strong and taut underneath her wandering fingers. He tilted his head back and closed his eyes, inhaling deeply at her touch.

She held her breath as uncertainty filled her. "Don't you want me to touch you?

Lucian's silvery gaze glimmered with unchecked desire. "Your touch is almost more than I can bear." He gave her a tight smile. "But I wouldn't have it any other way. Tell me what you want."

Was she dreaming? This felt so real. She may as well enjoy this while she could. Rana threaded her fingers through his hair, pulling his mouth to hers. "I want to finish what we started, Lucian."

His mouth captured hers in a hungry kiss. His chest flattened her breasts, rubbing her sensitive nipples through her nightshirt. In seconds, her shirt opened and his hair-roughed, naked chest grazed her bare rigid peaks. She moaned in response to the titillating abrasion.

Lucian pulled back, his eyes burning with need. He touched her breasts, squeezing them gently. "Your breasts are beautiful, Rana. They fill my hands perfectly." His words thrilled her beyond measure. He made her feel treasured.

When he twirled her nipples between his fingers, she gasped, arching her back, encouraging him, wanting to be closer…or…

He chuckled at her response and leaned over her, his warm breath fanning her breasts. "And these rosy nipples are just dying to be sucked." He drew a taut tip in his mouth, flicking it with his tongue before he surrounded the edge with his teeth and gave a gentle tug.

A swift ache surged between her legs, followed by hot moisture at the pain-pleasure she experienced. She rubbed against his thigh, needing the hard contact, the friction.

"Lucian, I need…" she panted, grasping his shoulders.

He slid his hand down her stomach and cupped her naked, quivering flesh, his expression suddenly intense. "Tell me what you need, Rana."

She bucked against his hand, seeking release from the building burn. "I need…you…now."

One long, warm finger slid inside her and she sighed in contentment at the magnificent feeling as his finger rubbed against her flesh. But he wasn't about to let her stop at contentment. Oh, no. While he trailed kisses down her stomach to her thigh, he moved his finger in and out of her moist sheath in a slow, rhythmic glide, causing her to lift her hips to match his pace.

A disappointed cry escaped her when he abruptly removed his hand. She came up on her elbows, ready to scream her frustration, but he surprised her when his strong hands grasped her thighs and pulled her closer, tilting her hips toward his lowering head.

"Lucian!" Rana put her hand on his shoulder and tried to back away. She'd never done this with anyone. But his grip on her tightened, his shoulders tensed, his expression full of longing, imploring her. "I need this, Rana. I want to taste you...all of you."

His words melted some of her resistance and before she could gather her thoughts, he dipped his head and found her throbbing core in one swift, decadent lap of his tongue.

"Luuuucian," she gasped, falling back.

He lifted his dark head, raising an oh-so-knowing eyebrow. "Shall I continue, my sweet?"

Rana nodded mutely, to which she received a wicked grin before he lowered his head once more and took a slow, tantalizing exploration of her sex, drinking her essence, lapping at her entrance before plunging his tongue inside.

She bucked in response, panting, clutching his head closer.

He made a growling sound and her breath hitched in her throat at the sweet passion building, intensifying with each sensual stroke of his tongue. "Oh, God, please," she begged.

Just when she thought she'd scream in insanity, he gripped her nub with his tongue and teeth and sucked hard. He pulled the responsive skin as far into his mouth as he could, eliciting a keening cry of pleasure from her for his efforts.

He chuckled and traced kisses to the juncture of her thigh as he replaced his tongue with two fingers, pushing deep inside her. "Please, Lucian," she pleaded, writhing at his magical touch, pressing closer.

"Come for me, Rana, long and hard. I want to hear you scream my name. Let me know it's my cock you really want driving into your sweet flesh."

He slid his thumb over her labia until it rested over her most sensitive spot while his fingers continued to twirl inside her. His fingers stopped moving and his thumb applied frustrating pressure as he slid his tongue over her thigh. She panted in agonizing anticipation.

His hot breath bathed her thigh before he gave a guttural growl and locked his teeth on the soft juncture at the same time he drove his fingers into her and pressed aggressively on her clitoris trapped beneath his thumb.

"Ohmigod, Lucian." Rana closed her eyes and gripped the sheets beneath her, screaming throughout her orgasm as her hips rocked with the most explosive waves of passion she'd ever experienced.

When she came back to herself, her eyes slowly fluttered open to stare at the dark ceiling. Disappointment coursed through her when she realized she'd had another tantalizing *dream*. Why did the most mind blowing orgasm she'd ever have end up happening while she slept? In her dream she'd felt connected to Lucian on a deeper level. His eyes told her what they shared was about more than just sex for him. Her heart still hammered in her chest, her body still pulsed from the pleasure she'd derived. Rana turned her head toward the window and saw Lucian's shadowy form.

* * * * *

Lucian reveled in Rana's uninhibited orgasm. He bit back the unfulfilled ache that radiated from his bulging cock. *Surely, I'm driving myself mad.* He chuckled inwardly. At least he'd thought to project the image of clothes around himself, so she couldn't see his amorous state. He wanted her desperately.

When she'd climaxed, it took all his will power to keep his fangs retracted and not sink them into her luscious skin. Never in his life had he wanted to taste a woman more. His passion for Elizabeth had built over time. But with Rana it was a fast, instantaneous flash and burn. Rana called to his most primal instincts to immediately mate in the traditional vampire way, to make her his for all time.

He should've known that sex would only heighten his need for her after this evening. In the parking lot, he'd come terribly close to taking her. Only her trusting voice calling to him, brought him back. Even then, he'd had to shake himself out of the haze of lust — for her blood as well as her body — that coursed through him.

He looked over at her panting in her bed and listened as her heartbeat returned to normal. Rana was like the flower and he was the bee. Even if his life depended on it, he couldn't stay away.

"Lucian?"

Rana stood on shaky legs, long, sexy, shapely legs that peeked out beneath her short silky nightshirt. She approached him, stopping a foot away, her hair tousled, her lips swollen from his kisses, the scent of her pleasure surrounding him in a cloud of pure temptation.

"Invite me in, Rana. I can't stay unless you give me permission," he whispered. He stared at her, letting her see the deep yearning in his eyes.

"I can't," she whispered back. The puzzled look on her face changed to one of determination as she reached out to touch him. Lucian shimmered before her hand could connect. She gasped and jerked her hand back to her chest, a sound of pure disappointment escaping her.

If she touched him, he'd be lost. He wouldn't be able to control himself. He was so primed right now, he'd yank her down on that bed and drive into her sweet flesh over and over while he sank his teeth in her neck. He reappeared across the room and asked, "Why?"

She walked toward him once more, reaching out. He shimmered again and solidified a couple of steps behind her.

Rana turned, smiling. "Obviously, you're not real and I'm still dreaming." She sighed and answered him, "I can't because I need to know what I feel for you is real — that I'm not covering my grief over my grandfather with a relationship."

Lucian closed his eyes for a second before returning her gaze. "I understand you've been through a lot with the loss of your grandfather."

Tears shimmered in her eyes. He couldn't help himself. Reaching out, he brushed her tears away with his thumb. "Don't cry."

She sucked in her breath at his touch and tried to reach for him, awe in her voice. "You're real." He didn't have time to vanish, so, he made himself an illusion instead, which drained him considerably. Her hand went right through him. She might not feel him but her gentle caress rocked him to the core.

Lucian gave her a tender smile. "When you're ready, I can be as real as you want me to be. All I want to do is love you, Rana."

Her smile was tremulous through her rain of glittering tears. "I could fall for you so easily, and that's what scares me the most."

Lucian shifted back to solid form and touched her cheek, brushing away another tear. He folded his hand inward and then opened his palm toward her. A single diamond, shaped like a teardrop, appeared in his hand.

She laughed, gulping back a sob. "Oh, Lucian, it's beautiful magic."

He smiled, cupping his hand around the diamond, his chest tight with his love for her. "There's so much I want to share with you, Rana. I'll be waiting."

Changing to his mist form, he left her smiling in the darkness.

* * * * *

The next evening, Rana entered her home and set the stack of books down on her coffee table. She stared at the book on top, amusement curving her lips. It was the book on vampires she'd shelved the other night. A customer had considered buying it but changed his mind at the last minute. When she started to put it away, for some unknown reason, she decided to take it home. She chuckled. At least no one could accuse her of not broadening her reading scope.

It was Friday night and she always brought home a set of books for the weekend. She giggled at her long-time habit and turned away from the tower of paperbacks. "Not tonight, guys. Tonight, I'm going to enjoy myself dancing with a handsome man." Shrugging out of her coat, she kicked off her shoes and marched back to her bedroom, mumbling, "So what if he's the hottie starring in my nightly fantasies. I can control myself."

She chose her outfit carefully, not wanting to seduce Lucian, but at the same time, she wanted to look sexy and alluring. The red pants suit's plunging neckline somehow enhanced her small, always-in-need-of-a-Wonderbra breasts, showing a modest curve of skin. The long sleeves were made of a see-through organza material that ended with a cuff made of the same rayon as the rest of the outfit.

Rana pulled her hair up in a French twist, sliding in pearl combs to hold it in place. As she applied clear lip gloss, the doorbell rang, causing her heart to flutter in her chest.

Lucian stood in her doorway, filling it with his tall, broad frame. He wore casual black slacks and a white turtleneck that fit his chest perfectly, displaying the show of muscle underneath. His short-cropped hair curled slightly, as if he'd just gotten out of the shower. A sexy smile tilted the corners of his lips. His silver eyes turned crystal clear, his smile broadening, when his gaze dropped to her outfit. Rana smiled and opened the door further, saying, "Come in."

Once she shut the door behind him, Lucian reached out and grasped her hand, lifting it to his lips. He raised his eyebrows hopefully. "We can always stay here and dance to the radio."

Laughter bubbled up. She felt giddy and drunk from his intoxicating gaze.

"Oh, no you don't. You promised me dancing, Lucian. No backing out," she admonished lightly.

He wrapped his fingers around her wrist and pulled her against his chest. "Your wish is my command. But first, a kiss."

Breathless, she could only stare up at him as he lowered his head to hers, his exotic scent surrounding her, seducing her. Sparks flew at the first gentle caress of his lips against hers. She gasped when he slid his hands down her back to her lower spine and pressed her closer, fitting her curves to his hard planes. His breath tasted of mints and something elusive, his own natural masculine flavor as he first nibbled and then sampled her bottom lip, running his tongue along the curve.

"You're like ambrosia, Rana," he murmured against her lips, "all sweet with just the right kick of citrus and mysterious ingredients to keep me coming back for more."

His words warmed her heart. Rana wrapped her arms around his neck and parted her lips. Lucian kissed her with demanding mastery, his tongue thrusting inside. He seduced her, enthralled her, took what she offered, yet insisted on so much more.

She put her hands against his chest, breaking the kiss. Knowing her eyes reflected her longing to continue, she pressed a finger against his lips with an apologetic smile. "Dancing, remember?"

Lucian kissed her finger, his eyes full of desire to please her. "Let's go. The dance floor awaits."

* * * * *

He parked his Jag outside a nightclub called *The Lion's Lair*. She turned to him, excitement in her voice. "I've heard of this place. It's supposed to be pretty exclusive and hard to get into."

Winking at her, he whispered conspiratorially, "I have an 'in' with the owner."

As they approached the door, the guard smiled at Lucian and opened the door for them. "Evening, Mr. Trevane."

"Good evening, Dwayne. Have you seen Ian tonight?"

"Yes, Ian's here."

"Good. By the way, as of today, Kraid is now banned from the club. "

The guard's gaze flicked to Rana before he addressed Lucian. "He'll be furious, sir."

Lucian tensed. "He forfeited his rights to this club by his recent activities. I won't tolerate such behavior."

Dwayne nodded his understanding. "No problem, sir."

Lucian put his hand on the small of her back and escorted her inside. Rana took in the swank establishment. A gleaming black marble bar took up one wall. Deep red carpet covered the entryway and the steps leading to the raised dance floor that took up the center of the room. People of various ages hung out around the French café tables surrounding the dance floor, while others took advantage of the lights under their feet and swiveled their hips to the latest hit song.

Curious about the conversation she'd just heard, Rana decided to focus on the obvious. She leaned over and said in his ear, "An 'in' with the owner, huh? You're the owner, aren't you?"

He gave her a sidelong smile. "Well, I didn't want you to think I was trying to impress you." His eyes lit up like a kid's seeking approval. "Did it work?"

Rana laughed. "You're incorrigible. Yes, I'm impressed."

A smug grin rode up his face. "Good. I like it when you're impressed." He nuzzled her neck. "Are you ready to finish what we started last night?"

She blushed, thinking of her dream, but remembering their shared kiss in the parking lot, laughed and swatted him away. "Slow down, Lucian. First things first. Let's dance, hmmm?"

He kissed her knuckles, his eyes alight with banked passion. "Yet another excuse to hold you close."

He pulled her onto the dance floor as patrons moved to the upbeat tempo all around them. The song ended right when Lucian and she made it to the middle of the dance floor. A Latin tune started up, its calypso beat thrumming through her veins.

Lucian lips brushed against her ear. "Have you ever danced the Salsa?"

She grinned. "No."

He put one arm around her waist, grasped her hand, and holding her arm out, he flashed her a smile. "Well, you're about to learn."

After a few mishaps, Rana had the basic steps down. Lucian was an excellent dancer. He smoothly directed, patiently taught, and seductively encouraged. Before the song ended, she had the swing of the dance. Disappointment coursed through her when the music ended.

"Did you like it?" Lucian asked.

She nodded. "I'm just disappointed that it's over."

He grinned. "Let wait and see, hmmm?"

When Marc Anthony's *I Need to Know* started up, she smiled at him.

Lucian pulled her against him and moved his hips with hers to the fast paced Salsa steps. Before long, they moved as one. It was as if she anticipated his next move before he made it and followed in suit. And the odd thing was, some of the twists and turns he'd adapted as they danced.

She locked eyes with his silver ones and became so focused on him, even the music seemed to dim in the background, the people gyrating around them faded way, leaving just Lucian and her on the lit-up floor, dancing to the sensual beat. At that moment in time her whole world centered on Lucian.

He pulled her closer until her chest touched his and said the lyrics as his lips brushed her neck, "I need to know".

At his suggestive tone her nipples hardened into tight nubs. Even the soft cotton of her bra felt almost painful as it brushed against them. It felt right with him — so right to just let go and enjoy the temptation, the pleasure he offered. She closed her eyes and relished the feel of his lips on her neck, his thigh between her legs, rubbing against her. Her thighs tingled in response to the hardness of his leg between them, reminding her of her first dream about Lucian and just how well he knew how to use that thigh. Rana's heart raced as her sex began to throb in pulsing need.

At some point, the pace of their dancing changed and slowed. Lucian slid his hands down her spine and grasped the curve of her ass in his palms, pulling her flush with his erection, rocking slowly against her. Rana bit back the moan that threatened to escape her lips.

His hot breath fanned her ear as he said, "You and I are in perfect harmony, Rana. I want to sink to the hilt in your warmth, bury myself so deep you come just from our joining."

Oh, God, he'd nailed it, big time. Rana couldn't stop her gasp this time. She was so turned on by his lurid words, the uncomfortable throbbing between her legs deepened to an unbearable, needy ache.

Lucian clasped her buttocks and lifted her off the floor, grinding against her. "I thought I could wait, my sweet, but you're driving me insane. Please tell me tonight is it."

The people were gone and it was just the two of them. She wrapped her arms around his neck at the same time she lifted her legs around his waist, letting her body settle on his erection. She moaned at the contact, reveling in the slight relief she experienced as he pressed against her. When he rocked his hips, rubbing against her once more, she imagined him driving his cock inside her as deep as he could get. Rana reflexively tightened her legs around him. She couldn't wait any longer either. She needed to feel alive and this time she wanted it to be real.

Her heart hammered in her chest, her breasts tingled, wanting his touch. "Yes," she whispered against his mouth just before she kissed him.

While they shared a kiss, the music came rushing back, the crush of people on the dance floor continued to swivel to the thumping music, oblivious to them.

Rana unlocked her legs from Lucian's waist and slid to the floor, heat rising to her cheeks at her uninhibited and very public behavior. She took a step back. What was it about this man that brought out the wild woman in her?

Lucian pulled her against him once more and planted a hard, branding kiss on her lips. He lifted his head and met her gaze, his own intense and searching. "Don't pull away from me, Rana. I couldn't bear it. Will you give me five minutes to speak with a friend before we leave?"

She nodded mutely and let him lead her away from the dance floor. A man with light brown hair approached them, his expression serious. "Lucian, we need to talk."

Lucian nodded curtly and introduced them. "Ian Mordoor, this is Rana Sterling."

The man's eyebrows lifted and he met Lucian's gaze before he shook her hand.

"It's very nice to meet you, Miss Sterling."

Rana shook his hand, enthralled by his charming smile and golden eyes.

Lucian turned to her. "Excuse me for just a few minutes." He indicated a barstool. "Have a drink if you like. I'll be right back."

Lucian and Ian walked away, talking earnestly. Now that Rana was alone, she had more time to think about her actions on the dance floor. Her cheeks flooded with renewed heat. Maybe some fresh air would help clear her mind. She jumped off the stool and walked toward the club's entrance. *I want this man more than anything. Now why does that thought scare the hell out of me?*

Chapter Six

"Kraid had help."

Lucian narrowed his eyes. "What do you mean?"

Ian clenched his jaw. "I found out that Kraid wasn't alone when he killed the vampire hunter. Drace was there. He helped torture the man before they killed him."

Lucian turned to face his friend. "Do I want to know how you came about this information?"

Ian grinned. "Let's just say you have two less Bruens to worry about and leave it at that shall we?" His smile faded and his eyes turned cold. "I'll take care of Kraid and Drace as well."

"No. Kraid is mine. He has to face the council."

Ian looked shocked. "But he might go rogue, disappear on us."

Lucian shook his head. "No, he won't. He thinks he did us a favor by killing the vampire hunter. The bastard's too arrogant to skulk away. He likes being the leader. Hell, he wants to be Vité."

"Isn't that a scary thought," Ian returned in a half-joking manner.

Lucian gave his friend a searching look. "There are those who will support his views on humans."

Ian laughed and clapped him on the back. "Yes, I'm aware the vote for Vité must be unanimous, but I know if anyone can convince the other leaders of the necessity for balance, it will be you."

Lucian nodded. "Thanks for getting the information. It should help with his dismissal as the Bruen leader."

* * * * *

Lucian walked back over to the bar where he'd left Rana. Her stool was empty. His heart jerked in his chest, fear gripping him. Where'd she go?

Lucian, I'm not real happy with you right now. Kraid's voice entered his head. He tsked continuing, *Banning me from the club. What were you thinking? I so enjoyed the willing donors I found there."*

For Kraid to speak in his mind, the conniving bastard had to be close.

Looks like you'll have to work for your food, Lucian replied as he headed for the door. Kraid had to be right outside.

Well, I guess I'll have to settle for what's right before me. He made a sniffing sound. *Mmmm, you smell good. Her blood smells sweet and pure.*

Lucian reached for the door handle, anger rising that Kraid would use someone so. He froze with Kraid's next words. *Just like the blood I smelled on you the other night.*

No! He can't have Rana. His heart dropped to his stomach, nausea a quick second behind.

In a flash, Lucian stood outside. Dwayne lay sprawled out on the ground, his head at a funny angle, his throat ripped out, while blood flowed from the gapping wound. Apparently, Kraid was being picky about his dinner tonight. He looked up and saw a group of college age men approaching the club. Thankful the hedge of bushes partially hid Dwayne's body, Lucian compelled the group to leave, making sure to include any others who might be near. He didn't need to deal with the police right now. He'd take care of Dwayne's funeral arrangements himself. Once the young men turned back toward their car, he quickly moved to the side of the building.

Kraid held Rana in front of him like a shield. "Nice of you to join us," he drawled as his hand fisted in her hair. He had her neck bent back to receive his bite, his teeth an inch from her throat.

"Lucian!" she screamed in terror, trying her best to pull away, but stiffening when Kraid's teeth hovered closer to her neck.

Lucian kept his expression calm while he spoke in her mind. *Rana, please be calm. I won't let Kraid harm you. Trust me.*

She whimpered. He could tell his speaking in her mind was freaking her out, too, but he needed her help to save her.

"I told you what would happen to you if you so much as thought about hurting my mate," he said in a deadly tone.

Kraid's laugh sent a chill down his spine. It was a crazed man's laugh, as if he were hyped-up on drugs. Nothing was worse than a vampire out of his mind. Not one remorseful thought would enter his thoughts as he went on a killing rampage.

Kraid's head snapped up, his eyes narrowed to glittering slits. "Do you really think I'm afraid of you, Lucian?"

Rana, when I say 'now', I want you to jerk free of Kraid's grasp and move away as quickly as possible. Blink if you understand me. He thanked his lucky stars when she blinked.

"You're hiding behind a woman, aren't you? he said, showing his fangs, letting a look of utter disgust reflect in his eyes.

Rana's gasp of shock permeated his bloodlust filled brain, sinking his heart. Now she knew the truth.

Kraid bared his fangs and hissed at him.

Now, he said in her head.

Rana stomped on Kraid's foot with her high-heeled shoe and ripped away from his grasp.

Lucian cleared the ten feet distance in a single leap, pouncing on Kraid before the vamp knew what hit him, sending them both to the ground. They hissed at one another, rolling on the pavement. He clasped Kraid's throat tight between his fingers, cinching them closed around it.

Kraid clawed at him, shredding the skin on his shoulders. Lucian slammed his fist into Kraid's chest, loosening the vamp's grip on his arms.

When Kraid's hand made it to his throat, Lucian decided he had played long enough. He dug his hand into the flesh and muscle of Kraid's chest, seeking his heart when the sound of screeching tires, followed by a dull thud, entered his consciousness.

Rana!

He looked up in time to see her body sailing through the air, hit by an oncoming car as she'd tried to run across the street. Guilt assailed him as he rushed to her, his fight with Kraid forgotten. She wouldn't have been running if it weren't for him and his vampire world.

He couldn't get to her side fast enough. As he crouched over her, he heard Kraid's gleeful voice in his head as he flew away. *Isn't it funny how life seems to repeat itself? First Elizabeth and now Rana.*

Lucian touched her pulse and finding none, roared his anguish at the sky.

* * * * *

Rana stood there staring at Lucian while he leaned over her body. The man who'd hit her had jumped out of his yellow cab and was babbling incoherently to Lucian. "I hit her. Oh, God. She just ran out in front of me. What have I done?"

Tears streamed down her cheeks. He's a vampire. He's a vampire. The words reverberated in her head. She'd finally found some happiness in her life and Lucian turns out to be a blood-sucking vampire. Life just wasn't fair.

A thin, older man walked up and stood beside her. He observed Lucian speaking in calm tones to cab driver who'd hit her.

She looked at the man beside her and stammered as she pointed to Lucian, "He..he's a vampire. I...I just saw him leap ten feet in the air. He's got fa...fangs and red eyes. And...and oh, God, I guess that means he drinks people's blood."

The man put a hand on her shoulder and said in a calm voice, "I know, Rana. Calm yourself."

Her fears suddenly disappeared. Her mind registered the fact that Lucian was a vampire from a logical perspective instead of an emotional one. She stared at the old man. He didn't look like an angel in his blue jeans, red sweater and a baseball cap over a thatch of silver hair. But how else could she explain the feeling of calmness that passed over her at his slight touch and unhurried command?

Lucian reached over and felt her pulse. He wouldn't find one. She realized with a wry smile, she was dead. Now that she knew the truth, her blossoming relationship with Lucian was over. *Which is probably a good thing because I think he and I would've had two entirely different views on the expression, 'dinner for two'. I'm fine with being an appetizer, but not the main course.* A morbid, but happy thought struck her. Her death meant she'd be able to see Jack again.

The man next to her looked at her and shook his head. "You're too eager to die, Rana. You must go back." He spoke as if he'd read her mind.

"No. I died." She gasped at his words. The idea of seeing Jack again held great appeal right about now.

He smiled and his wrinkled face became even more creased. "Technically, you're not dead. You're in limbo. You must go back, Rana. Lucian needs your help."

She sputtered as anger rose within her. "But...but you're an angel. Why would you want me to help him?" She gestured toward Lucian, refusing to acknowledge the sadness in his face as he looked down at her. "He's evil."

He gave her a patient look. "I'm not an angel. I'm a...Gatekeeper...of sorts. Do you know what the name Lucian means?"

She shook her head.

"It means 'Man of Light'."

At her confused expression, he sighed and explained, "Even the darker side has varying degrees of evil, Rana. Lucian is the light in the darkness that is his race. And that's what vampires are—a race of people called Kendrians. Lucian's leadership is needed, but he resists. You need to help him find his way and accept the position of Vité at the vampires' council meeting in two days time."

When she started to interrupt, he held up his hand and continued, his blue eyes meeting hers. "But in order to accomplish this task, you must remain pure until he takes the oath of leadership."

She'd been watching Lucian stroke her face as the man explained her task. At The Gatekeepers last words, she shifted her gaze back to him. "Pure?"

He nodded. "Yes. You mustn't let Lucian make you a vampire."

She laughed, rubbing her neck to keep away imagined neck bites. "No problem there, Mr. Gatekeeper. I like the sun too much and the idea of drinking blood makes me nauseous. Plus, who wants to live forever?"

His chest rumbled with his suppressed laughter. "Vampires do eventually die. They just age very slowly, over centuries."

She looked at him. "If I do this? If I help Lucian, then I'll die?"

The man nodded. "I can't change what has happened, Rana. But Lucian needs someone to help him right now."

She set her lips in a firm line. "Okay, I'll do it." Putting her hand out, she asked, "But could you remove this ring before I go back. The scent it emanates seems to…um…attract him quite a bit." Her cheeks flushed in embarrassment.

The old man smiled, shaking his head. "No, I'm sorry. You have to go back as you came. I can't interfere."

"You already have," she snapped. "You're sending

me back." Even though she was angry, her heart ached when her gaze landed on Lucian bending over her, rocking her body in his arms, holding her close.

"Such vehemence from someone who wanted to die two seconds ago." The old man chuckled.

She flicked her gaze back to him. "Hey, you'd be a bit ornery too if you'd just discovered vampires exist, been hit by a car and killed, only to find out you can't die yet, because you have to go help a reluctant vampire become the leader of his people all the while keeping those fangs at bay. Yeah, I'm seeing life through rose-colored glasses, no doubt about it."

Before he sent her back into her body, The Gatekeeper told her, "I'll heal your wounds, since you can't very well help Lucian if your pelvis is crushed."He grinned at her shocked expression before he continued, "How about we skip the listing of your internal organ injuries."

* * * * *

Rana sucked air into her lungs in one long gasp. Lucian looked down at her, his expression shocked. "Rana?" He touched her cheek and then slid his hands over her arms and legs as if looking to see if anything was broken. "It's a miracle," he whispered, returning his gaze to her face.

Rana jerked from his grasp, scrambling away from him like a crab, wincing in the process. Man, she was going to be one big walking bruise. *Hey, Mr. Gatekeeper, I thought you'd heal all my wounds. I hurt like hell!* She looked at her burning leg where the asphalt had torn her pantsuit. A streak of road rash dotted her thigh. Moving her hand to touch it, she noticed a gash on her palm as well. *Okay, so maybe the hell comment wasn't the best choice of words.*

"You're hurt." Lucian reached for her again, but she shrunk away, her eyes wary.

The wounded look in his eyes went right to the pit of her stomach, but she needed to be strong. He'd led her to believe he was something he wasn't—a normal human being.

As if he'd read her thoughts, Lucian spoke softly, "Rana, I'm still the same man."

She slowly stood up on shaky legs. "No, you're a vampire. A little something you forgot to mention to me." Angry with herself for even caring one smidgen that she was hurting him, she looked around and noticed they were alone on the road.

Spreading her arms wide, she said with sarcasm, "Well, isn't that just lovely, the guy who hit me just took off and there are no witnesses to boot."

"I told him to go home."

She looked at him in surprise. "What? And he just listened to you?" she asked, taken aback. Then it hit her—scenes from all those old vampire movies ran through her head. "You compelled him to leave, didn't you?"

Lucian nodded, regarding her with watchful eyes, gauging her reaction.

She started to ask, but she stopped herself, thinking, *What's the point?* Technically, other than a few bruises, she was fine. After rubbing the dirt off her torn pants suit, she put her foot back in the shoe she'd lost while flying through the air and turned to limp back to the nightclub, intending to call a cab.

"Rana, I want you to come home with me where you'll be safe," Lucian called from behind her.

Rana stopped and turned back to him, laughing. It was either that or breakdown in hysterics. "Safe from whom? Kraid?"

She walked right up to him, meeting his gaze head on. "What about you, Lucian? When you get really hungry, are you going to take my blood, too?"

The insulted look in Lucian's eyes, before he masked it with a blank stare, made her regret her harsh words. She waved her hand wearily and said, "I'm sorry. Being hit by a car has a tendency to make me a little crabby. Can you just take me home?"

He pressed his lips together in a firm line and nodded as he pulled his cell phone out of his pocket. He called Ian and asked him to take care of Dwayne.

Great, that gorgeous Ian guy was a bloodsucker, too? Rana shook her head as she followed him to his car.

* * * * *

Lucian walked Rana to the door, expecting her to slam it in his face. She said over her shoulder as she walked across the threshold, "Come in and take off your shirt."

He wasn't sure he understood where she was going with her request. She seemed angry, not amorous. He stood outside her door, wary, studying her.

"Come on." She waved him in as she walked down the hall.

Lucian pulled off his shirt, grimacing at the gouges on his shoulders. He followed her into the bathroom.

She pointed to the closed commode. "Sit."

He lifted an eyebrow at her imperious tone but complied without comment.

Rana pulled down alcohol and cotton balls from the cabinet above the sink. He grasped her wrist when she moved to apply the cleanser to his wounds. "I'll heal just fine, Rana."

She met his gaze, her own fearful at his touch. He realized her tough act and sarcastic comments were bravado. She was terrified of him. Sarcasm and anger he could deal with, but this…this fear from the woman he loved, it stripped him bare.

He rubbed his thumb over her wrist, holding her gaze. "It's me, Rana, Lucian, remember?"

Her pulse beat faster underneath his finger and she closed her eyes. Was it from fear? With all his vast powers, the one he didn't possess—the ability to read minds—he'd kill for right now just to know what she was thinking.

Rana's eyes flew open. She jerked her hand from his grasp and put the alcohol away. When she turned back, she refused to look at him again. "You can go now."

"Rana."

She closed her eyes once more and said, "Just go, Lucian."

He set his jaw as he stood. "I'll leave your home as you requested, but I won't leave you unprotected."

Lucian pulled on his shirt and walked out.

*****

As soon as she closed the door behind him, Rana leaned against it and sank down to the floor, tears flooding her face. She cried until her head hurt.

Wiping away her tears, she lifted her head, sniffling. She'd begun to really care for Lucian. For that matter, if

Kraid hadn't interfered, she'd have already slept with the man. She sighed. *I guess I should be thankful for 'evil-guided' favors.*

Rana stood up on unsteady legs and headed for her bedroom to change into a gray sweatshirt and navy lounging pants. She returned to the living room and flipped on the light. She was too keyed up to go to bed just yet. Eyeing the stack of books, her gaze landed on the book on vampires.

How timely, she thought with an ironic smile. She reached for the book and sat down to read. If she was going to help Lucian, she had to learn everything she could about vampires.

After a couple of hours of reading, she felt she understood his vampire race a little better: they have little, if any tolerance to sunlight, they must drink blood to survive, they have the ability to make the donor forget they'd given blood, they're incredibly strong, they can turn a human into a vampire if they take blood from the person three times within a few days time, and oh, yeah, vampires might not be immortal, but they live for centuries, so they may as well be.

She yawned and looked at her watch. It was one in the morning. Standing up, she stretched and turned off the lamp. As she passed the bay window, she noticed a man's outline leaning against the glass. Lucian. He'd never left.

She unlatched her door and leaned outside. He turned his head her way. "I said go home, Lucian."

His arms folded at his chest, his ankles crossed in a casual stance, Lucian's gaze remained steady on hers. "And I told you I'm not leaving you unprotected."

Rana flipped her hand. "And what are you going to

do when the sun comes up? I'm assuming you can't handle full sunlight, am I correct?"

Lucian slowly nodded his head.

There was no way she'd be responsible for another death today. Her own was enough. She sighed and beckoned him with her hand. "Come in, then."

Lucian flashed a smile and moved toward her.

"But you have to leave as soon as it's dark tomorrow night, understand?"

He nodded as a small smile remained on his lips. She gritted her teeth at his knowing look and walked back to the guest bedroom.

Rana was conscious of his heat as he followed behind her, the animal magnetism that emanated from him. Her skin flushed and a shiver passed over her as her heart rate picked up, its steady beat changing to a more fervent pace at his nearness. His step was so quiet she didn't know he was so close behind her until she opened the door and turned to him.

"Here's your room—"

His hard chest brushed against hers, making her very aware of her taut nipples underneath her sweatshirt. The vampire thing may throw her mentally, but her body still reacted to him. Lucian put his hands on her upper arms to steady her. She hadn't bothered turning on a light, so only the moonlight lit up the hallway, casting it in an ethereal glow.

He reached up and touched her cheek, his fingers lingering at the edge of her jaw line. Rubbing his thumb across her lower lip, he said, "Good night, sweet Rana."

Rana swallowed, nodded, and walked to her bedroom. As he started to shut his door, she poked her head back out into the hall. "Oh, the window has a room darkening shade on it. It's pretty much pitch black with the shade down."

Lucian smiled his appreciation. *Thanks for thinking of me*, he whispered in her mind. The mental contact was both intimate and seductive.

"Don't do that," she snapped, straightening her spine. She quickly pulled her head in and shut the door behind her.

* * * * *

Lucian sat on the bed in the guest bedroom and leaned against the headboard. He heard Rana washing her face, brushing her teeth. He could smell the toothpaste she used as it mixed with her own innate scent and his cock hardened in response to the stimuli. He leaned his head back and listened to her soft sigh as she pulled the covers over her sweet body, heard the glide of the sheets against her silky skin.

Rana was so much more than he ever could have hoped for in a mate. She wasn't beautiful in a classical sense, but her face still drew him in. He delighted in her inner strength and her wicked sense of humor. After today's horrors, he wanted to hold her close and conquer all her fears. He lay back on the bed, mourning the loss of tonight—what should have been their night together.

* * * * *

Kraid had her pinned to the ground, his fangs exposed. "When I'm done draining your body, I'll rip that lovely neck of yours to shreds," he sneered. "What's Lucian going to do with a dead corpse, hmmm?" Kraid leaned closer; she couldn't move. All she could do was scream at the top of her lungs. "Lucian!"

"Shh," Lucian said soothingly against her temple as he held her in his arms. "It's okay, I'm here, Rana. It was just a dream. Nothing can harm you."

Rana clung to him, the remnants of her dream, the fear, the terror, still very real in her mind.

Lucian ran a calming hand down her hair, rocking her in his arms. Finally, the tremors stopped and his stroke turned more sensual than soothing. Rana closed her eyes and drank in his intoxicating, masculine smell. He'd removed his shirt, but he still wore his pants. His skin felt warm against her. Here in the dark, she didn't have to look into his eyes and be reminded he was a vampire. She imagined he was the Lucian from her dreams even if just for a few moments.

His hand dropped to her shoulder and touched the strap of her nightgown, sliding it down her arm, his lips tracing its path. Heat curled in her belly, and adrenaline kicked into high gear setting her heart at a rampant pace.

"Your skin is so soft," he murmured against her shoulder.

She put her hand on his bicep, reveling in the feel of his hard muscles.

He took her hand and stroked his tongue against the gash on her palm, before he set it on his bare shoulder. Reaching for her breast through the silky sleep shirt, he urged the bud to a hard, sensitized peak with a gentle brush of his fingers. Rana gasped at his touch, thrilling at the vibrations thrumming through her body. It felt so good when it was real.

Wait! What was she doing? She couldn't do this. Rana

stiffened and pushed his hand away.

"Rana, I care for you very much. Please don't let this change us."

His plea broke her heart. She closed her eyes, unable to face his tortured expression or her own tumultuous emotions.

Lucian cupped her face in his hands and touched his lips lightly to hers. Her body ached for him, his heat, his touch.

But she was on borrowed time. She couldn't let herself fall for Lucian. Nor could she let him believe they'd have a happy ever after. It was best to let him think she didn't care for him.

She pushed him away, saying in an unaffected voice, "Thank you for rescuing me. Again. Good night, Lucian."

He stared at her. It was hard to read his expression in the dark, but she thought she saw hurt and anger in his eyes. He lifted himself from the bed and stood beside it for a long agonizing moment. She waited, holding her breath. If he pushed her, she didn't think she'd be able to resist him.

"Good night, Rana." He turned and walked out of her room.

* * * * *

Anger coursed through him. He wanted her. She wanted him. He knew she did. But she pushed him away. Why? Because he was a vampire?

Well, being a vampire had its advantages, too, he thought as he settled into the bed and let a wicked smile ride up his face. There was no reason they shouldn't have their night together. He leaned back against the headboard, closed his eyes, and worked his magic.

Because of their deep connection, it was easy to share his feelings of desire with Rana. He smiled at her gasp when she felt the clawing, pit-of-the-stomach need he experienced. Lucian concentrated on her soft skin, her sensitized nipples. He brushed an invisible tongue across one and then the other. By the audible gasp and thudding of her racing heart, he knew exactly when the throbbing desire took hold of her. *Spread your legs. Let me touch you. Your hand is my hand*, he whispered on the edge of her mind. Not enough so she would know it was him, but enough to push her over the edge.

He shuddered when she touched herself and he heard her moan. To know she was in the other room, rubbing her damp labia, sliding her fingers inside—a place he so desperately wanted to be—almost did him in. He freed his shaft from his pants and stroked himself in the same rhythm of her rampant breaths. His heightened sense of smell caught the scent of her arousal and the seductive aroma hit him hard. He tightened his jaw as his own pace on his cock increased with hers.

Lucian imagined the hand that touched her throbbing clitoris was his hand and the fingers that sunk into her wet sheath were his, that it was her hand that held him in a firm grip, knowing exactly what to do to get him off. And she did, in a way. When her muffled cries of ecstasy reached him, Lucian felt his balls tighten as her feelings, so strong and pure, permeated the walls between them. His mind reached out and absorbed her emotions like a sponge, reveling in both the real and vicarious sensations the link between them allowed as he finally surrendered to his own explosive climax. *You're mine. My anima*, he whispered along the perimeter of her mind, right before she fell asleep.

Chapter Seven

The next morning, as soon as Rana opened her bedroom door, Lucian opened his. They stood there staring at one another for a tense, heart stopping moment.

"Good morning." He finally broke the silence. The lines around his eyes and mouth made him look tired and even more dangerous.

Rana knew she couldn't look much better. When she woke up, her entire body ached. She felt like she'd been hit by an eighteen-wheeler, not some rinky-dink yellow cab. She didn't bother with niceties. "You look terrible. Did you sleep at all?"

"No. I told you, I must protect you."

"It's daylight now, Lucian. Surely, you can give yourself a break."

He slowly shook his head, a determined expression on his face. "Kraid will only rest for a little while. He'll discover you didn't die in that accident and come looking for you."

Her brows drew together. "Why would he come looking for me?"

"Because of me." Lucian sighed as he ran a hand through his hair. "He knows how much I care for you..."

"Don't say that." She cut him off.

He looked surprised by her comment. "Why?"

"Because we can never be, Lucian." She turned and

walked down the hall.

His strong hands were on her shoulders, turning her around before she'd taken three steps. "Because I'm a vampire?"

She winced at the pain his sudden movements caused, drawing in her breath.

Lucian let her go, his eyes apologetic. "I'm sorry, Rana. I forgot you don't heal at the same pace."

Rana was thankful he'd been distracted from his question with his thoughts of her welfare. But his statement peaked her curiosity. She reached over and pulled his torn shirt away from his shoulder. There were no deep gashes, only faint lines.

She met his gaze. "Amazing."

He grinned. "Being a vampire does have its advantages."

Rana let go of his shirt and turned away in a huff, angry that he could be so flippant. Kraid played for keeps. And from her reading, she knew vampires weren't invincible.

Without thinking, she closed all the curtains in the house before she walked into the kitchen. Once there, she opened cabinets, pulled down coffee and slammed them closed in her frustration.

"Want some coffee?" she grumbled over her shoulder.

"Sure," Lucian said from the doorway.

As Rana set up the coffee pot, she felt the weight of Lucian's gaze on her back. She opened the fridge and pulled out bagels and cream cheese.

"Why can't we be, Rana?" he asked softly as he sat down at the table.

Rana set out coffee cups and poured him a cup, adding two teaspoons of sugar to his. Leaving the spoon inside the cup, she set his on the table with a thump.

"Because you're a vampire," she stated bluntly, hoping that would get him off her back.

His expression unruffled, Lucian took the spoon between his fingers.

She watched him stir his coffee, thinking, *three circles to the right and one circle to the left,* and Lucian did just that.

He regarded her with a thoughtful expression as he lifted the cup and took a sip. When he set the cup down, he gave her a broad smile. "You knew just how I like it."

Rana opened her mouth to deny his statement but was thoroughly confused as to why she'd put sugar in his coffee without asking, why she didn't think to ask him if he wanted cream, when somehow she knew he wouldn't. And then there was that whole stirring thing. How strange.

"I'm going to take a shower," she said, grabbing her bagel and turning away. She ignored his chuckle as she stomped down the hall.

* * * * *

Rana returned to the living room an hour later. She'd taken her time with her shower, needing the distance from Lucian's disturbingly magnetic presence.

She found him sitting in her reading chair with the book on vampires in his hands. He lowered it when she entered the room.

"This book is filled with all kinds of inaccuracies," he said in an arrogant tone.

Rana raised an eyebrow and sat down on the soft brown leather couch, curling her feet underneath her. "Oh, really? Well then, care to enlighten me?" She couldn't have engineered a better way to ask Lucian about his race without seeming entirely too interested.

Lucian opened the book and drew his finger down the page. "Here. It says you can detect vampires because they have no reflection in mirrors. That's not true." He flipped some more pages. "Here, it says we hate garlic." He looked up and met her gaze. "That's not true." Thumbing further into the book, he reached another section. "It says we can't abide the cross. A cross is just a religious symbol, no more, no less."

He turned a few more pages and read, "'Vampires can only be killed with a wooden stake driven through their hearts.'" He rolled his eyes. "Give me a break." He looked at her once more. "Hey, I bleed. If you cut something off, it stays off. Yes, I can be killed in various ways."

Rana shuddered at his words. And yet he didn't disagree with the drinking of blood, the aversion to sun, the superhuman strength, the ability to move faster than the eye can see, the almost-immortality, the night-vision, etc.

She leaned forward, needing to know for certain. "So you don't disagree with the rest?"

He shook his head. "No, some of it was right on."

She looked at her watch and then faced him, gulping for what she was about to ask, but he looked worse now than he had earlier. "Don't you need to eat?"

His smile was tender. "Yes, but I can wait."

Rana shook her head at his stubbornness and grabbed a book off the stack she'd brought from the store. Settling into the contours of her sofa, she sat back and opened it. Lucian smiled at her and reopened his as well.

After a couple of hours, she noticed the slant of the sun coming through the bottom of her curtains. It was two in the afternoon and she'd skipped lunch.

Jumping up from the sofa, she looked at Lucian. "I'm fixing a sandwich, do you want anything?"

When Lucian looked up from his book, his eyes were slightly glazed, his expression very tired.

"Are you okay?" she asked in alarm.

Lucian snapped out of his haze and looked at her, his face set in hard lines as if he were holding back pain. "I'm fine."

"No, you're not," she insisted. "It was daylight when I saw you at the graveyard. How early can you go out?"

"It depends on how overcast it is. If it's a sunny day, I have to wait until at least five in the afternoon."

Rana folded her arms. "When five o'clock rolls around, I'm kicking your vampire butt out of my house. You need to feed, Lucian. I don't want your health on my conscience."

He set his mouth in a firm line. "If I'm able to be out and about, so is Kraid." He gave her a steely look. "I'm not leaving you. Period."

Rana walked away, shaking her head at his bullheaded attitude. She mulled over Lucian's protective nature while she ate her sandwich. It both thrilled and worried her. He's said he cared a great deal for her. The thought saddened her. Why did he have to be a vampire and why did she have to be dead? Once she'd eaten, Rana made a sandwich for Lucian.

Setting it down on the end table near his chair, she said, "Eat something, please."

Lucian flicked his gaze to the sandwich. "Thanks for thinking of me, but blood is my only food source."

"But you drank coffee earlier."

He smiled. "That was purely recreational. I don't need it to survive."

Rana sighed with frustration and sat down, picking up her novel. Well, she tried at least.

* * * * *

Lucian's entire body shook with his need to feed. He bit back the clawing hunger and instead focused on Rana. Her blonde hair fell forward as she bent over her book. He watched her delicate hand absently brush the strand away from her face and tuck it behind her ear.

He adored her pert nose, her wide set eyes and expressive eyebrows. He loved her full lips when they quirked upward in humor, her strong sense of self, even in the face of near-death. Even her dedication to her grandfather's memory made him want her more. He wanted to see that kind of dedication in her expression when she looked at him. Instead, he saw uncertainty, anger, and betrayal reflected in her eyes when she cast her gaze his way.

Lucian closed his eyes as his strength weakened. Normally he could go for weeks without eating if he was in a deep sleep, but having to constantly deflect Rana's scent so Kraid couldn't detect her, drained his energy considerably.

He sunk further into the chair and clenched his jaw as the sound of Rana's beating heart and the whooshing pulse of her blood pumping through her veins grew louder.

* * * * *

After another hour had passed, Rana lifted her gaze when Lucian's book dropped to the floor. His face was very pale, his entire body tense.

She rushed to his side, but he quickly jumped up from the chair and moved over to lean against the front door, closing his eyes. "Stay away from me, Rana. My body is craving blood and I don't trust myself around you."

Rana stood up and looked at her watch. It was only four. He still had another hour to go. While she contemplated what to do, Lucian slid to the floor, landing on his butt with a soft thud.

"Lucian!" She squatted next to him, heedless of his warning. Rana touched his forehead. He was so cold. "Lucian, you must eat."

He lifted his head and whispered, almost in delirium, "I hear your blood rushing through your body, Rana, so sweet and warm."

Rana closed her eyes. She had to help him. She couldn't bear to watch him suffer. *But I'd better confirm the three strikes you're out rule.* "How many times, Lucian?"

"Mmmm?" He looked at her, confused.

She grasped his shoulders. "How many times does a human have to be bitten to become a vampire?"

"Three close together," he mumbled.

"Good. Then once won't kill me."

His eyes closed and she panicked, her heart racing in fear. Pulling him close to her, she offered him her neck.

"Take my blood, Lucian. For God's sake, take what you need to survive."

Lucian looked at her neck and his nostrils flared. He set his jaw and shoved at her, sending her sliding back across the wood floor. His expression was intense and the most focused she'd seen him in the last few hours.

"No," he said forcefully. "When I take your blood, it will *not* be for sustenance."

His words sent a secret thrill racing to her stomach, but she didn't have time to contemplate his meaning. Rana scrambled to her knees and placed her hands on her hips in anger. "Don't be ridiculous, Lucian. I'm here, willing to give you what you need."

His eyes lost focus again and this time his head fell back against the door. He was talking to himself. "I must keep the house camouflaged."

She crawled to him and shook his shoulders. "Is that why you're so weak?"

His head drooped and his chin touched his chest. He mumbled something unintelligible.

She hit his shoulder as tears streamed down her face. "Don't you dare die on me from something so stupid, Lucian. When this is all over, I'm going to kill you myself for being so stubborn."

Rana's mind scrambled for something to do. Then it hit her. The word Lucian had said sounded like Sabryn. Could the Sabryn she'd bought the ring from be his sister? She rushed to her purse and pulled out the receipt from the antique store.

Her hands trembled while she dialed the number and waited for an answer.

"Hello."

"Sabryn?"

"Yes."

"Sabryn, my name is Rana Sterling. Do you have a brother named Lucian Trevane?"

"Yes," she said breathlessly. "Is my brother okay? I didn't see him last night. I've been worried sick."

Rana quickly explained what happened. "Lucian's being stubborn and is now close to passing out on my living room floor. I'm afraid for him."

"I'll be right there. Give me directions to your home."

* * * * *

Twenty agonizing minutes later, someone knocked at her door. Rana grabbed Lucian's hand and tried to pull him away from the door, but Lucian clasped her wrist in a vice-like hold, stalling her efforts.

"No. Don't open your door."

Rana said in her most soothing voice, "Lucian, it's Sabryn. I called her."

His hold tightened, but his eyes couldn't stay focused on her, they lolled in his head. "No. It's a vampire trick."

Rana called to Sabryn through the door. "Sabryn, please speak to your brother mentally. Let him know it's you. He won't let me open the door.

She waited for a few tense seconds and finally Lucian's grip loosened as he collapsed to the floor, completely unconscious. Rana tugged him out of the way, doubled-checked through the peephole, and then opened the door.

Sabryn rushed in, an older gentleman with black hair sprinkled with gray, followed in her wake.

"Lucian," Sabryn called out, concern etched in her beautiful features as she bent over her brother and touched his cheek.

Rana watched in amazement as the woman lifted Lucian in her arms as if her were a mere child. She walked out the door, calling behind her, "Uncle Vlad will stay to protect you, Rana."

Rana sank to the floor and let the tears fall. *God, please don't let it be too late for Lucian.*

* * * * *

Sabryn took him to a secluded park and compelled three humans, two females and a male, to them. With a worried look, she left him to nourish himself. He fed until he was completely satiated. Tonight, he did erase the memories of those who'd given him their blood. He hadn't been violent, but he hadn't the time or inclination to lure and cajole as he normally would.

Strength surged through his veins as he shapeshifted to a raven's form. Lucian's heart pounded in anticipation now that he was assured of Rana's love for him. He'd stubbornly stayed by her side, needing to protect her from Kraid, his soul sinking to the deepest despair over the condemnation in her eyes whenever she looked his way.

But before he lost consciousness, he'd seen the concern written all over her face, remembered the anger and then alarm in her voice when she yelled at him for being so foolish. Rana cared. She cared a great deal. He sucked the fresh air into his lungs, reveling in life as his heart filled with happiness.

When he neared her house, anger and revenge coursed through him, dampening his high spirits as his mind turned to Kraid. The evil bastard was out there, waiting to try and kill her again. Did Kraid have something to do with Elizabeth's death? He couldn't forget the vamp's words of 'life repeating itself'.

Now that Rana knew him for what he really was, he refused to hide anything about himself from her, ever again. Lucian misted into the living room and materialized, stark naked, right in front of Rana as she stood up from the couch. Sabryn cast an amused glance his way, his uncle's expression stayed deliberately neutral, but the look on Rana's face turned to one of shock.

"*That* certainly wasn't in the book," Rana said, keeping her eyes at his shoulder level and above.

I only said the book had some inaccuracies. I didn't say the book wasn't missing a few pertinent facts, he stated dryly in her mind.

Her face drained of color before a fusion of embarrassed pink tinted her ashen pallor.

"All those nights? You were real?" She narrowed her eyes on him.

"Lucian…" his uncle started to speak in a warning tone.

Lucian spoke to Sabryn and Vlad in a clipped tone, never letting his gaze leave Rana's. "Leave us."

His relatives walked out the door, leaving him to contend with her wrath.

*　*　*　*　*

He stood there, handsome, strong and virile, nothing like the unconscious man she'd screamed at and cried over a couple of hours ago. And there was something else in his commanding stance. Power. Power rolled off of him in waves. Lucian's metallic eyes met hers, his expression thoroughly unrepentant, almost pleased with her reaction.

Her heart stopped in her chest when, in a matter of seconds, she relived all they'd done, all she'd shared with him. Fury fueled her accusatory words. "You stole into my most secret thoughts, Lucian. How could you?"

He pressed his lips together and took a step toward her. "I can only speak in your mind, Rana. I can't read your thoughts. What I know," he spread his hands as if absolving himself, "you shared with me willingly."

Rana held up her hand to speak and then turned her back to him. "Cover yourself, Lucian, I can't talk to you this way."

Lucian chuckled. "As you wish." All of a second passed before he said, standing right behind her, "You can turn around now."

Rana peeked over her shoulder, doubtful he'd be able to accomplish the task so quickly. Lucian wore a white turtleneck and jeans.

She turned back around. "How did you...? Where did you get...?" Finally, she gave up wondering. *What the hell, nothing made sense anymore anyway.* She let her expression turn cold and distant and crossed her arms over her chest. Tilting her chin up at a defiant angle, she responded to his absolution of his duplicity. "I shared with a character in a dream."

He scowled and angry lines formed around his mouth. Grasping her arms, he yanked her against him. "You shared with your *lover*, Rana." Stormy gray eyes searched hers. "Because that is what I am, your lover."

His words shot right to her lower belly and below, causing a pure, primal reaction within her. Her sex throbbed and her nipples pebbled, making them so sensitive even her bra rubbing against them set her on edge. Rana put her hands on his chest to shove away from him, needing the distance to keep her composure, and gasped when she touched skin, not clothes.

"Your clothes are an illusion?"

Lucian nodded with a solemn look.

Rana backed away and began to pace in an effort to clear her mind. She'd come so close to losing him. Her heart soared to see him healthy and vibrant again, but her chest constricted when she realized what she'd shared with him was real—that the man knew exactly how to make her fly apart at the seams.

"In my mind you were an illusion." She stopped and faced him. "Not who you really are."

He stepped close to her, reaching out to touch her face. Tenderness replaced the anger in his eyes. "I'm the same man, Rana. My desires haven't changed. I only want to love you."

She closed her eyes at his words. The hurt they brought, especially now that she had so little time left, tore at her heart.

He cupped her face in his big hands. "I want you to come home with me."

Her eyes flew open. "What?" She backed away from his touch, shaking her head. "No, Lucian."

He lowered his hands and spoke in a low, even tone. "You're life is still in danger, Rana. I can protect you better if you're with me. I have guarded my house against vampires." He swept his arm around her living room. "You're vulnerable here, open to attack."

How would she be able to resist him if she was constantly around him? She shook her head once more.

A determined expression settled on his visage, his dark brows slashed downward. "You're coming with me, Rana. It's your choice, come willingly or I'll compel you. I care not which."

Suddenly, the memory of him talking to the cab driver, telling him everything was okay, came rushing back. He'd told the man, to go home and the driver had complied, without questioning him, without repeating the need to call an ambulance. Had Lucian done that to her as well? Was everything they'd shared a lie?

Her stomach clenched in knots, but she needed to know. When she spoke, her voice shook, "Is that what you did to me in my dreams, Lucian? Compelled me?"

His eyes locked with hers, the cadence of his words mesmerized her as he beckoned her with his hand. "Come to me."

Of their own accord, her feet took her to stand in front of him. She remembered walking toward him but not why she did so. He stroked her jaw with his thumb, a smile lingering on his lips. "Now you know what it feels like to be compelled, sweet Rana. I've never compelled you. Not once."

She knew the truth of his words. What she felt during their love making, her actions, were her own. She remembered every vivid, sensual detail.

He lifted her hand and kissed her palm reverently. "I need you with me, by my side. I have a council meeting to attend tomorrow, but I won't go unless I know you're safe."

The council meeting had to be the one The Gatekeeper spoke of, the one where Lucian was to become Vité — leader of all the vampires. After seeing just how evil and powerful vampires could be, she supported Lucian taking on the role. Rana closed her eyes and swallowed. *I can do this, I can do this and keep him at bay,* she chanted to herself. When she opened her eyes and met Lucian's determined gaze, she heard Jack's amused voice, *You know you're dead meat, don't you?*

But what else could she do? She nodded. "I'll go with you." At his smile of approval, she held up her hand. "At least until you attend your meeting." He didn't need to know she wouldn't be leaving his home. Dying could put a real damper on one's desire to stay and redecorate.

Chapter Eight

Rana stared in awe as Lucian drove up the long driveway leading to his house. His home was a beautiful mansion, set atop a hill, and surrounded by acres of rolling green pastures. The white house sported no less than thirty windows along the front, each adorned with fancy black shutters. Two huge columns supported the front entrance. A gurgling fountain graced the center of the circular driveway.

When Lucian pulled the Jag up to the front of the house, a tall man walked out and opened Rana's door for her.

"Good evening, Miss. Welcome to Trevane Manor," he said formally.

Rana resisted the urge to say, "Bloody good evening to you, too," figuring the butler would think her humor in poor taste. She stifled a giggle at her own 'punny' ridden thoughts and instead mumbled, "Good evening." Where was this morbid humor coming from? Maybe she was really suffering hysterics and she didn't know it yet.

Or maybe you're finally just enjoying life. She heard Jack's voice in her head.

Too little to late, I'm afraid, Jack.

Lucian grasped her elbow and walked her across the threshold while the butler pulled her suitcase from the car. Rana stood inside and stared at the tall walls full of artwork—some of which she knew had to date back a few centuries.

The main hall had a vaulted ceiling with four wide black marble columns supporting the bulk of the ceiling's weight. The columns sank into a beautiful black, white and maroon tiled floor. Beyond the four columns, two curved staircases flanked the back of the room on either side. The staircases led to the second floor and a balcony that overlooked the entire room.

When the butler walked past, Lucian called out, "Jeffery, please put Miss Sterling in the west wing near me."

Rana quickly looked at him but didn't have a chance to comment as two huge black and gray wolves approached, their wary eyes focused on her.

Involuntarily, she shifted closer to Lucian. Lucian clasped her hand and held her palm out for the wolves to sniff. He spoke to them soothingly. "Jet, Rune, this is Rana. Welcome her to Trevane Manor, boys."

Rana willed herself to remain calm. After all, Lucian was right next to her. Surely the wild beasts wouldn't attack her with him near.

"Wolves are a vampire's best friends. Even though we can sense another vampire, they can sense a presence before we can and alert us to danger, which is especially important while we sleep."

"They seemed to listen to you. Can you talk to them in their minds, too?" Rana asked quietly as the two wolves sniffed her hand, wetting her palm with their noses.

Lucian nodded. "Yes, I can touch their minds, but only if they aren't alpha wolves or werewolves. But that also means so can other vampires."

"Werewolves!" Rana turned to him. "Werewolves really exist?"

Lucian laughed at her shocked expression. "Yes, but we keep our distance from one another, for obvious reasons."

"What, two powerful forces going head to head?" Rana's lips twitched in amusement.

"Something like that." Lucian chuckled. He continued where he'd left off. "Alpha wolves' minds can't be touched by a vampire and that's what makes them very prized among vampires — they can't be quieted or told to remain calm by another vampire. They do as they please, which, if one comes to live with a vampire family, he will protect that family as if it were his own pack. But such creatures are hard to find and usually won't come close to a human or a vampire."

Rana giggled at the tickling sensation when Rune snorted in her hand. After sniffing his fill, Jet sat back on his haunches and panted, but Rune wasn't done. Before she could react, he lifted up on his powerful hind legs, threw his paws over her shoulders, and licked her cheek.

Rana laughed and grasped the wolf's huge face in her hands as he continued to lick her. "Whoa there, Rune, buddy." She turned twinkling eyes to Lucian to see him staring at her with a stunned expression.

"What? You told them to welcome me."

Lucian spoke, his voice low, almost in a whisper, "I've never seen a wolf do that, Rana. Ever."

"That's because you picked the right mate," Sabryn said as she walked down the stairs and called the wolves to her.

Both animals immediately moved to flank her on either side while she approached with an amused expression.

Rana stiffened at her words and looked at Lucian. "Mate?"

"Good night, Sabryn," Lucian said in an annoyed tone. Clasping Rana's elbow, he propelled her toward the stairs.

Rana pulled from his grasp as they walked up the stairs. "Mate?" she repeated again, giving him a sidelong look.

When he didn't answer her, she said, "Lucian, I don't want you to get the wrong impression as to why I'm here. I didn't want you to miss your important meeting because of me. That's all."

While she talked, they'd turned down a long hall. After passing several rooms, Lucian finally stopped and opened a door.

He smiled. "Here's your room."

"Did you hear me, Lucian?"

"Yes, I heard you." He touched her shoulder before she walked in. "Are you hungry? It's well past dinner time for you."

Rana walked into the room and turned to face him. "No, I'm just tired. I think I'll take a bath and go to bed early tonight." She stretched her arms. "My muscles are still a little sore from yesterday."

"It's pretty amazing you survived that accident with barely a scratch." He grinned. "Must've had a guardian angel looking out for you."

You have no idea, bud. This angel only gave me time, not a get out of jail free card. Nope, didn't get to 'pass go' or 'collect $200'.

Rana decided to change the subject before he delved deeper. She'd never been a very good liar. She asked with a grin, "So, where's your coffin?"

Lucian smirked. "Very funny."

She spread her hands wide. "Well, help me out here. The book I had obviously wasn't the best. I figured you could fill in the blanks."

He crossed his arms and leaned against the doorframe. "I sleep in a bed, just like you." A devilish grin rode up his face as desire reflected in his eyes. "Even better, I could sleep in your bed with you." Lucian's clothes, or image of clothes, blinked before her eyes. His broad muscular chest came into focus, reminding her his clothing was nothing more than an illusion.

Rana turned her back to him, refusing to acknowledge his proposition and grumbled, "For Pete's sake, go put some real clothes on, Lucian."

Lucian walked off chuckling. "Good night, sweet Rana."

She shut the door and heaved a sigh of relief. Good lord, how was she going to remain 'pure' with *that* running around, tempting her every five minutes?

Rana decided a bath would help her to relax before she went to bed. As she entered the bathroom, she gasped in pleasure at the beautiful room. Stark white tile with dove gray accents lead to a gorgeous claw-footed bathtub—the outside deep burgundy and the inside snow white.

She walked over to the tub and turned the gold lever handles, looking forward to a long, hot soak. While the water ran, she slipped out of her clothes and pinned her hair up with a clip she'd brought from home. Rummaging through the cabinet, she found some bubble bath and poured a capful of the clear liquid in with the running water. The scent of gardenias suddenly filled the room.

Rana moaned in pleasure as she sank into the warm water. Leaning her head back, she closed her eyes and realized this might very well be her last pleasure bath before she died. As her thoughts drifted down that morbid path, she felt cool air brush against her nape.

Lucian stood in the doorway, two fluffy burgundy towels in hand. His gaze skimmed the surface of the bubbles as if hoping to get a glimpse of her naked flesh. "I thought you might need these since you mentioned taking a bath. This bathroom isn't used very often so I didn't know if there were any towels in here."

Thankful for the bubbles surrounding her, Rana said, giving him a sheepish smile, "I was so excited to find this wonderful tub, I didn't even think beyond getting in. Thanks."

Lucian pulled the delicate gold stool with a white seat cushion close to the tub and laid the towels on it along with a bath sponge. Was the sea sponge his? she wondered.

Rana noted he'd changed clothes. Or, put clothes on rather, she thought with an inward chuckle. Now he wore a dove gray fine gauge Merino wool v-neck sweater and casual faded jeans. God, how did the man manage to look delicious in just about anything he wore? The sweater only made his eyes look even more like liquid pools of mercury.

He squatted by the tub and tapped the end of her nose with this finger. "Need any help with your back?"

Rana's cheeks burned at her traitorous thoughts. She wanted him to pull his clothes off and join her in the tub. Hell, she didn't care if it would be a tight fit. That'd just give them an excuse to snuggle closer.

She closed her eyes and bit her lip before she voiced her thoughts. When she opened them to decline his offer, Lucian already had his sleeves pulled back and had dipped the sponge in the water.

Steam rose up from the water and the scent of gardenias filled the air between them while Lucian awaited her response. *This may be the last time he'll touch me.* With that thought, Rana leaned forward slightly and said, "Okay, thank you." Before he could move she placed her hand flat on his chest.

At his raised eyebrow, she pulled her hand away, leaving behind a wet handprint, and said, "Just checking to make sure you really did put on clothes." Good grief, the last thing her libido needed was to know he was as naked as she while he bathed her back. Lucian chuckled and she waited in anticipation as he moved behind her.

When the sponge slid down her back, its touch so soft, she knew in her heart the sponge was from his personal bath. The thought that he'd share such a personal item with her made her weak in the knees and ever so thankful she didn't have to stand at the moment because she knew she'd be unable to.

"My God," Lucian swore, low and fluently. "Your body really took a beating, Rana. These bruises are every shade in the rainbow." His words came out hushed as if he really couldn't quite believe she'd survived the accident unscathed.

Rana had completely forgotten about the plethora of bruises covering her body. She immediately straightened and leaned back against the tub, saying as she held her hand behind her head for the sponge, "I think I'm good now."

Instead of handing her the sponge, Lucian bypassed her hand and slid the sponge down her chest, dipping it straight into the water and rubbing her breast from the inside curve to the tip. Rana sucked in her breath at the sensations she experienced as the soft material slid across her hardened nipple.

Pure, remember? I know it's kinda hard with all those lustful thoughts clamoring around in your head, Rana, but you have to remain pure, she told herself. *What do men do when faced with pure temptation?* she wondered. *Oh, yeah, they think about sports.*

Rana straightened her shoulders and concentrated while Lucian moved the sponge to her other breast. *Football. A touchdown is worth six points and a field goal is worth one, but wait, the field goal could be worth three points if—* All 'good intention' thoughts fled when Lucian's lips grazed her neck, causing her skin to pebble.

She gasped and he immediately let go of the sponge and cupped her breasts in his hands. Rana tried to lean forward, but he pulled her body flush with the back of the tub and nipped gently at her earlobe.

When he twisted her nipples between his fingers, heat curled in her belly and Rana moaned, arching her back instinctively, pressing her breasts into his hands. Her body screamed for her to give in to the passion Lucian offered. No-no-no-no-no-no-no, she couldn't let him do this to her.

He'd be like one potato chip and she'd never in her life been able to just eat one.

Rana pulled his hands off her breasts and sat up in the tub, crossing her arms over her naked breasts, "Good night, Lucian." After a long pause, he sighed deeply.

She refused to look at him when he finally said, "Good night, Rana," before he closed the door behind him.

* * * * *

"Hmmm, you smell so good," Lucian inhaled, whispering in her ear, his breath warm against her skin.

Lucian's deep baritone voice skittered across her nerve endings, setting her on fire.

Rana arched her neck toward him, inching her body closer.

"Wake up, Rana."

Rana opened her eyes. Lucian leaned over her, his hands held her wrists above her head, his body braced over hers. She met his intense gaze, noted his bare chest, and felt the heat of his naked leg searing her hip as he sat beside her on the bed.

"This is no dream. I'm here in flesh and blood." Lucian said as he let his gaze rake down her flimsy nightgown, stopping on her nipples thrusting against the thin silky fabric. His nostrils flared when he returned his gaze to hers. "And I want you very much."

Rana bit her lip and shook her head, but gasped when she felt an invisible hand tweak her nipple, pulling it against the fabric. She arched at the sensations his mental touch elicited. She started to speak and an invisible warm mouth closed over that same nipple sucking it deep. Rana whimpered as desire shot straight to her sex, making it throb in unfulfilled need. Her gaze met his and drifted to his mouth. Oh, lord she wanted it to be real.

Lucian's lips canted in the corners as if he read her mind. He mentally slid his tongue down her abdomen until he planted a kiss on her mound. Rana clamped her legs closed, trying desperately to thwart his torturous onslaught. Lucian kissed her jaw at the same time he slid an invisible tongue against her swollen clitoris. *Make him stop. Any way you can or you'll pass the point of no return.*

"Another vampire power, Lucian?" She gasped, trying to gather her thoughts. "I read that you're supposed to ask permission—that a vampire can't come into a person's home unless he or she is invited," She panted the words out as she felt her clit manipulated by an invisible mouth. She involuntarily sighed in pleasure. "This isn't playing fair."

He raised a dark eyebrow and gave her a rakish grin. "You're in my home now, my sweet. I don't have to ask permission." His expression turned seductive. "But I will. Let me in, Rana." He leaned close and said near her ear as he mentally slid his tongue around her labia, "I want to come into your home, over and over."

The double entendre sent a thrill thrumming through her, tightening her nipples, making her ache to know just what it felt like to have him inside her, just once. Rana searched deep within herself to find the strength to resist his enticing voice and tantalizing tongue. "Let me up, Lucian."

He sighed and released her wrists. Rana scrambled away, hopped off the bed, and turned her back to him. She couldn't look at his perfect, naked body. It was too beautiful for words. She'd fallen asleep with the bedside lamp on, and now the bulb's soft glow illuminated his broad, muscular shoulders and powerful arms, the dark hair that slid into a vee at his navel, giving way to trim hips that lead right into thick corded thighs.

She closed her eyes to shut out the mental image in her head, but she immediately sucked in her breath when she felt his heat directly behind her. Lucian's chest touched her back and he said against her neck, "I know you want me." Inhaling, he continued, "I smell your arousal, your sweet, feminine scent calls to me, Rana." His lips grazed her neck and Rana let her head fall back against his chest.

It's so hard to be good, she thought. *I want to taste the passion.*

Lucian's strong hands turned her around. His smoky gaze locked with hers as he cupped a hand around her neck and pulled her closer until her breasts touched his hard chest.

"Surrender all your dreams to me. Let me love you," he said in a low voice right before his lips met hers in a tender, searching kiss.

She sighed and melted into him, no longer able to resist his magnetic lure. Lucian smiled against her parted lips and slid his tongue inside, slanting his mouth over hers. Placing her hands on his waist, Rana returned his kiss, stroke for delicious stroke.

Lucian groaned and pulled her closer, deepening the kiss, drawing her further under his provocative spell. His hands slid down her back and grasped her backside. Molding her soft curves to his hard body, he pressed the heat of his erection against her belly and whispered in her mind, *No more dreams. No more vicarious sensations. I want to explore your body to the fullest first-hand.*

Rana shivered at his words. She ran her hands up the corded muscles in his back, reveling in the strength underneath her fingers. *Just this once, I want to feel the desire between us and know it's not a dream.*

Lucian fisted his hand in her hair and tilted her head back while he ran his lips down her jaw to her throat. Rana shivered in delight as he nibbled on the sensitive curve between her neck and her shoulder.

"You taste so good, Rana," he said in a husky voice.

A sense of déja' vu brought on by his words caused a pleasant shudder to pass through her. Then she remembered where she'd heard him say those words before. He'd said them in her first dream about him. Cool air greeted her breasts as Lucian lowered the straps on her silk nightgown. The fabric whispered down her body and pooled around her feet on the soft carpet. He continued his kissing path down her chest, pausing to kiss each nipple, and then moved on to her lower belly to tease her navel, before he bent down on one knee and slid her underwear down her legs.

Rana touched his head and thrilled at the feel of his silky hair between her fingers. Her heart pounded in her chest and she waited in anticipation for his next move.

Lucian grasped her ankles and drew her legs further apart. He ordered gently, "Open to me, Rana, love. I want to touch all of you."

She slid her feet further apart, her breathing turning uneven while his hands made slow, methodical massaging trails up her legs until he reached her inner thighs. Lucian splayed his fingers around the muscles, leaned closer, and blazed a hot trail with his tongue from her lower inner thigh to the juncture at the top of her leg. His warm breath fanned her already heated skin as he made his way back down to her wet curls. Grasping her thighs, he pulled them further apart and grazed her moist lips with a purposeful swipe of his tongue.

Rana's moan turned into a startled gasp when Lucian made a low growling sound in his throat and clasped her to him, lifting her bodily off the floor. She yelped, grasped his head for support, and wrapped her legs around his waist as her entire body tilted backward toward the carpet.

Expecting to land hard on the floor, she instead stopped an inch from the carpet, her fall cushioned by air. Slowly, her body lowered for a soft landing.

Her heart hammered in her chest at the experience. She chuckled. "Another vampire power you forgot to mention?"

He gave her a wicked grin before he dipped his head and gave her another lap with his tongue, this time right against her clitoris. Rana arched off the floor as a keening sound of pleasure ripped from her throat.

Lucian lifted his head, his eyes reflecting his banked passion. He pressed on her thighs. "Relax your legs. I want to look at you."

Rana did as he asked and let her legs fall to the floor, opening to him.

He smiled, pulled her lower lips apart and inspected her thoroughly. "You are so pink and wet." He slid a finger straight down her slit. Rana whimpered her need.

He raised an eyebrow. "Do you like that?"

She nodded.

Lucian shook his head, *tsking*, "No, Rana love. Tell me. I want to hear the words." He pressed on her throbbing clitoris.

She panted in tense anticipation.

"You're clit is plump with your desire." He circled the sensitive bud with his finger and then met her gaze once more. "Tell me," he demanded.

"Yes," she gasped at the steady pressure he applied, lifting her hips, seeking release from the building torment. "I want you inside me."

A purely satisfied male smile tilted the corners of his lips and he thrust a finger deep into her. Her breath hitched in her throat while sensations of pure pleasure rippled through her. He moved closer, leaning over her to capture a nipple in his mouth as he added another finger and slipped them both inside her while his thumb pressed against her clitoris.

He kissed her breast tenderly and lifted his head to look into her eyes as his hand continued its masterful manipulation. "Come for me, Rana," he said, plunging into her. Her breath escaped in short, unsteady pants while her hips canted to meet his hand's rhythmic movement. She closed her eyes at the building sensations.

"No," he said, his voice low, controlled. "Don't close your eyes, Rana, I want to see your desire unfold."

Rana bit her lip and then smiled at him. She placed her hands on his shoulders and arched once more when his thumb moved in smaller circles over her throbbing nub. "Lucian," she breathed out his name as the first ripples of her climax built within her body, tensing her stomach, accelerating her heart rate.

"Say my name again, Rana," he whispered, his expression intense.

No need to prod her there. Her body gripped in the throes of delicious climatic spasms, Rana screamed out his name, "Lucian!" as her moist, highly sensitized sheath contracted around his stroking fingers again and again.

When her body stopped quivering, Lucian leaned closer, kissing her neck. He inhaled deeply, drinking in her scent. "You thoroughly seduce me," he sighed.

Rana gave a throaty laugh and wrapped her arms around his neck while he nuzzled hers. "I think the exact opposite is true, since I'm the one who just climaxed."

"Oh, I'm not done, yet, my love." Lucian looked at her, his dark brow elevated, a wicked smile on his face.

Rana gave him a siren's smile. "Lord, I hope not."

He chuckled, lifted her in his arms and walked toward a side door. Pulling it open and then kicking it closed behind him, Lucian carried her to his bed. Rana's heart filled with joy at the room. It was beautiful. Even through Lucian had all the window's drapes pulled closed, there was hidden lighting in the ceiling that lit up the room as if it were daytime, the warmth and feeling the glowing light conveyed was as close to sunlight as you could get.

His elevated four-poster bed was made of a smooth honeyed wood, the posts thick and intricately carved. A pure white comforter covered the bed, matching the mostly white décor around the room. Certainly not what she expected from a creature of the night. While Lucian held her, Rana did the honors and pulled back the covers, gasping in surprise. The blood red silk sheets underneath were such an incongruent contrast she looked up at him and asked with a smile, "Do you have a split personality, Lucian? Something you want to tell me?"

Lucian gave her a devilish grin. "A man has to have his small pleasures in life, something to look forward to."

God, that sounds just like something Jack would've said. She smiled at the thought, knowing Jack would've liked Lucian, vampire and all.

Lucian gently laid Rana on the bed and stared down at her. With her blond hair spread out on his red sheets, her hazel green eyes filled with desire, she made a beautiful, tempting picture. His chest contracted with love. Before he could lie down beside her, Rana reached out and wrapped her warm fingers around his cock, a knowing smile on her face. Her small hand felt so good around him, he clenched his jaw to keep from losing it right then and there. Lucian clasped her wrist in his hand.

"I'm feeling a little guilty that all this has been about me." She sat up and curled her legs under her. Lucian's hold tightened when she leaned over and licked the moisture from the tip of his cock. "Mmm, you taste good."

He closed his eyes and groaned at his body's instantaneous response to the slightest touch from her tongue. His stomach tensed, fisting into knots, and his balls tightened as his cock hardened even more, if that was possible. Lucian had never been more aware of his desire for a woman in his entire life—only one woman. Elizabeth may have helped him find her, but Rana was his true mate.

As she stroked his cock with her mouth and talented tongue, he became acutely aware of every pulse of blood flowing through his body; he heard Rana's blood rushing through her veins, smelled the scent of her arousal. All his senses heightened at the seductive combination.

He opened his eyes and pulled her up to her knees, his voice sounded gritty and strained, even to himself. "Enough, love."

She met his gaze, disappointment in her eyes. "But I want to…"

Rana didn't get to finish her sentence before his lips captured hers in a possessive kiss. She cried out in delight when he pushed her back on the bed and knelt over her.

She placed her hands on his strong shoulders, sliding her fingers over his bulging biceps, appreciating the dips and hollows of his chest above her. Lucian rested his body over hers. His pale gray gaze met hers and locked as he settled his thighs in the cradle of her hips, pressing his erection against her heated entrance.

She smiled and spread her legs, welcoming his hard shaft as he slid into her. A fleeting thought occurred that they should be using protection, but she dismissed it. *Why bother, I'm already dead. I may as well live while I can.*

Rana moaned as her body stretched to accommodate his large size.

"God, you're so tight and full of hot cream," he bit out, his body tense while he slowly guided himself into her.

She could tell he was holding back his desire to ram home. Rana smiled. "Then we'd better do something about it." Before he could respond, she wrapped her legs around his waist, lifted her hips upward, and pulled him toward her.

Lucian flashed a wicked smile at her invitation and drove into her in one swift thrust—a thrust so deep he touched her womb. "Ohmygod," she called out as her body immediately climaxed at the thorough invasion.

Lucian called her name in a hushed tone. Rana opened her eyes and met his passionate ones as her sheath finished contracting around him. He held himself very still until all her tremors had stopped.

Giving her a tight smile, Lucian set his jaw and began to move. Using slow methodical thrusts as if he meant to heighten her pleasure, he kept his breathing even and measured. Rana would have none of it. He'd held back his own pleasure too many times for her. She arched her back, lifted her hips and met each of his thrusts with counter ones of her own, upping the stakes, increasing the pace.

Sensations built, curling within her lower stomach. Her breasts and thighs tingled, her sex begged for more friction, harder pressure. Lucian's lips captured hers, his ravishing kiss matching the fevered rhythmic pace of his hips grinding against hers.

Rana gloried in their passionate lovemaking. Her breasts brushed his chest, aching and sensitive against the hair-roughed surface. Lucian trailed his lips down her neck, tasting her with his hot tongue.

Her breathing became erratic as her body hummed and prepared for another climax. Rana strived to get there, but at the same time, she didn't want it to end. She dug her fingers into his shoulders, begging, "Please, Lucian."

Lucian pistoned into her and clamped his teeth on her throat. Rana arched her back and tilted her head, crying out, "Lucian, yes! *Yes!*"

When the first shimmers of her orgasms started, Lucian gave a deep guttural growl of satisfaction and sunk his teeth into her neck, pulling her closer as he took her blood. Rana gasped in pleasure as the intense, erotic act heightened her climax, making the heart-stopping spasms seem to last forever.

Lucian reveled in Rana's blood—untouched by another—pure and sweet. He drank like a vamp with his first taste of blood. She tasted so good, he had to stop himself before he took more than her body could recoup in a day. Regretfully, he withdrew his fangs and gently licked her neck, closing the wounds.

Rana's hands moved slowly over his back. She seemed lost in a trance.

Apprehension gripped him. What if he accidentally took too much of her blood? Lucian grabbed her shoulders and shook her slightly. "Are you okay, Rana love?"

Her eyes came back into focus and she smiled. "Wonderful. Just tired, that's all. I had no idea love making could be so intense and erotic."

He cupped her face in his hands. "So, you're okay with me taking your blood during our lovemaking?"

"Yes, so long as it doesn't happen again…" Rana trailed off with a tired smile, her eyes closing in sheer exhaustion.

Lucian gathered her sleeping form against his chest and pulled the covers over them. He knew she'd sleep for several hours, since the first time was usually the most exhausting. Her last comment concerned him. She knew it took three encounters before she'd become a vampire. And once she became his mate, the exchange of blood during lovemaking was one of the most sensual aspects of being a vampire. Why would she not want that? Rana said she enjoyed their intimate act. The question plagued him

before he finally succumbed to his own fatigue and fell
into a deep sleep.

Chapter Nine

Rana awoke to the smell of bacon. Her stomach growled in response to the strong aroma. She slid out of bed, careful not to wake Lucian. He needed his sleep more than she did. She took a moment to appreciate the rich royal blue and white tile floor and coordinating blue glass containers that graced the white marble counter top in the bathroom before she hopped in the shower.

Once she was dressed in casual black slacks, a white tank top and a royal blue cardigan, she quietly made her way downstairs. As she descended the curved staircase, Rana noted it was almost dusk outside. Wow, she had been exhausted. She'd slept almost twenty-four hours. No wonder she was starving.

A young girl, who looked to be about sixteen rolled around on the floor at the bottom of the stairs, wresting with Jet.

"Hello," Rana said in a friendly voice when she reached the bottom step.

The girl jerked her head around, her chin length, flaming red hair bobbed with her movement. Her smile disappeared from her face as if she was ashamed to be caught enjoying herself. She eyed Rana up and down and sniffed the air. "You're not one of them, are you?"

Rana laughed. "No, I'm not a vampire. I'm just here visiting. My name's Rana."

The girl nodded, looking back at the front door as she rubbed Jet's head. "Yeah, me too. I'm busting out of this looney bin as soon as I'm old enough."

Rana started to ask the girl her name when Sabryn walked up beside her.

"Good evening, Trish. Did you sleep well, dear?"

Trish cast a cutting look at Sabryn. "How can you ask me that? You weirdoes have my body all messed up. Making me sleep during the day, keeping me awake all hours of the night. Bunch of freaks," she muttered under her breath as she turned back to Jet.

Sabryn ignored her comment and said in an upbeat tone, "I believe Uncle Vlad is setting up the chess board in the study."

Trish was up and running before Sabryn finished the last word. "See ya later, Rana," she called behind her.

Rana's heart went with her. She missed her chess games with Jack.

"Trish's parents were killed in a car accident. Her mother was one quarter vampire and her father was half werewolf." Sabryn explained the girl's behavior, shaking her head. "She doesn't realize how special she is. She hasn't come to the age of awareness yet."

Rana looked at Sabryn in surprise. "You mean she doesn't know she's from two very distinct races?"

"Right. Because her parents were neither a full vampire nor werewolf, their lives were very much like humans." She sighed. "We aren't sure what powers Trish will develop, but we don't want a rogue vampire or werewolf trying to take her for his own. So, we brought her here." She gave a brief smile. "For some reason, she's taken to Uncle Vlad."

Rana laughed. "It's the chess games. My grandfather had me addicted."

"Good evening, Rana love," Lucian said in her ear from behind her. He placed his warm hands on her shoulders and gently squeezed.

Rana stiffened at his words but couldn't keep herself from inhaling. He smelled woodsy and clean at the same time, his skin still warm from his shower. Rana turned to look at him as Sabryn stepped into the foyer and addressed her brother with an amused expression.

"You're looking quite rested this evening, Lucian."

He grinned and let his hand slip around Rana's waist as he stepped down to the last step beside her. His silver eyes twinkled as he looked at her, but addressed his sister, "Yes, I think a whole day of sleep was just what we needed."

Rana's embarrassed blush spread all over her body. Okay, *now* his sister knew they'd slept together. If she could speak in his mind at the moment, she'd tell him off, but good. Instead she excused herself and followed her nose toward the dining room and the wonderful smell of bacon.

Lucian put his hands on her shoulders and turned her around right before she walked into the dining room. "What's wrong, Rana?"

"Wrong?" She gave him an incredulous look and surveyed the room to make sure no one was about before she spoke in a lowered voice, "You basically just told your sister that we'd slept together."

Lucian laughed and rubbed her shoulders, giving them a gentle squeeze. "You're my mate, Rana. It's expected."

The deep baritone of his laughter was easy and pleasant and she would've enjoyed seeing him so happy if she weren't so miserable—by the end of the evening, he'd be Vité and she'd be dead. "Lucian, I told you already. I'm not here to become your mate."

"You can so easily dismiss last night?" His fingers tightened on her shoulders and the look of hurt in his eyes was almost more than she could bear. She had to be strong. But she couldn't lie to him either.

"No, Lucian. Last night was spectacular, but becoming a vampire would change my entire life. I'm not ready for that." Okay, scratch the goody-two shoes theory. She could lie—when necessary. Before he could reply, she twisted out of his hold and entered the dining room.

A woman wearing a maid's uniform came out of the kitchen with a carafe of coffee and set it on the table with a friendly smile. Her short gray hair bushed against her cheeks as she turned and said, "The food's on the sideboard, dear," before returning to the kitchen, leaving her alone.

Rana noticed Lucian enter the dining room, but she ignored him as she filled her plate with bacon, eggs and hash browns. He sat across from her as she set her plate down. Man, was she hungry. She'd taken several bites when Lucian said quietly, "Now that I've found you, I can't imagine my life without you, Rana."

Rana paused the fork midway to her mouth at his words. She met his steely gaze. "Lucian…" she began.

His eyes burned with intensity as he continued in a husky voice, "I want to fall asleep with you in my arms every morning for the rest of our lives."

Her heart ached at his words. He was saying all the right things. God, make him stop, please—"Stop."

Rana felt a set of hands lay heavily on her shoulders. She immediately turned, but no one stood behind her. She shifted her gaze back to Lucian and narrowed her eyes.

He spoke in her mind instead. *I want to taste your sweet flavor again, feel your body wrap around mine, hear you screaming in pleasure.*

The hands slid past her arms to touch the sides of her breasts before skimming down her waist and hips. Slowly his fingers slid across the crease of her legs before they touched the juncture between her thighs. Tiny shivers started in her chest and shot down to her stomach before settling in her sex. Rana dropped the fork and jumped up, slamming her hands on the table between them, rattling the plate and silverware. "Stop it, Lucian!"

Lucian stood and leaned across the table, his hands bracketing hers in, the lines in his face taut with fury, his silver eyes sparkling in anger. "I will not! You are my mate, Rana."

That commanding presence was back. The dominance he exuded shot down to her stomach and sizzled right back up her spine, leaving her weak and breathless, making her want to punch him square in the nose and kiss him senseless at the same time.

"Well, you're just going to have to…"

"Lucian…" Sabryn interrupted her as she entered the dining room. His sister let her gaze dart back and forth between them and said, "I'm sorry to interrupt, but the clan leaders want to meet with you to discuss Kraid before the ceremony."

"Now?" Lucian sounded frustrated.

"Yes, they're gathered in the library." She turned to walk out, but glanced back, eyeing them. "I'll tell them you'll be a minute."

Lucian's gaze returned to hers. "Finish eating, Rana. I want you to come, too."

Rana looked at him in surprise. "Why do I need to be there? It sounds like a private matter."

He straightened and rubbed his hands on his neck, saying, "You're my mate, Rana. You go where I go."

When she opened her mouth to object, he continued, "Plus, I need you to tell them what Kraid did to Dwayne and tried to do to you. Do you think you'll be up to it?"

She straightened her shoulders, nodded, and sat down to finish her meal.

* * * * *

After she'd told her story about Kraid, Rana sat in a cushioned chair next to the door, listening to the clan leaders talk. She felt out of place among them, being the only woman. Well, Sabryn was there, but she was a vampire and the sister to the man about to become Vité, so she had her own station of importance.

At least she knew the names of the clans now. Lotta good it'll do her, Rana thought wryly. But she let her gaze follow the men around the table nonetheless. There were: the Kantrue's led by Lucian, the Bruens led by Kraid, which Ian represented tonight, the Norradors, the Arryns, and the strangest, the Sythe. Their leader was bald with squinty eyes and pointy, *yes* pointy, ears.

The leaders argued among themselves as to how to punish Kraid—whether or not to make an example of him before they killed him. The vampire law, she learned, was not like humans'. They took care of their own rogue vamps. The court system and due process was happening in this room right now. The argument had turned so heated, Sabryn stepped in to calm the men down. Rune moved over to sit beside her, leaning against her leg. Rana reached out and rubbed his head.

Suddenly, the wolf's entire body tensed. He looked at her as a low growl escaped, but then the sound changed to a whimper.

Are you ready for me, Rana? A voice entered her mind. Kraid.

Her entire body tensed and she looked at Lucian who was debating with the Arryn clan leader.

What, no answer? That must mean Lucian hasn't made you a vampire yet. Maybe he's having second thoughts, since you don't look anything like his fiancée, Elizabeth.

Lucian's eyes met hers for a brief second, but she looked away before he could see the pain and confusion Kraid's words brought.

Kraid made a *tsking* sound. *So tragic, Elizabeth's demise. Lucian mourned her death for months until he decided to foolishly believe in reincarnation.* His harsh laugh grated on her nerves. *What cockamamie bullshit! Can you believe he thought that ring would bring her back to him — that he thinks you're Elizabeth reincarnated?*

Rana looked down at the ring on her hand. God, now it all made sense. Elizabeth's grave was the one Lucian was visiting that day in the cemetery. He'd told her he was saying good-bye. Now she knew why. That was the day he saw her.

She closed her eyes as the hurt and betrayal washed over her. So what if she'd be dead before sunrise. The knowledge didn't stop the anguish that tightened her chest. Rana covered her mouth with a trembling hand to stifle her cry as she bolted from the room. Lucian called to her, but she ignored him and headed straight for the front door. She had to get away. She thought she was strong, but she wasn't strong enough to handle this.

Rana didn't make it past the water fountain before something knocked her roughly to the ground. The cement scrapped her side through her clothes as she skidded across the unforgiving surface.

Kraid was on her before she could move. He pinned her to the ground and grabbed a fistful of her hair, yanking her head back, exposing her throat for his impending bite. She knew he intended to tear her to shreds. His bright red eyes blazing, his fangs extended, he hissed out, "You're the reason I'm not being voted Vité tonight."

"Me?" she managed to strangle out the word.

"Lucian had no interest in the Vité position until you showed up. He wouldn't have challenged me." Kraid lowered his head closer to her neck.

As scared as she was, Kraid's arrogance and cowardice infuriated her. Rana drew on the knowledge she was already dead to give her the strength to fight Kraid the only way she could. By pissing him off. Letting her anger take over, she kept her voice calm and taunted, "You're not the sharpest fangs in the clan, are you?"

At her sarcastic words, Kraid jerked his head up and met her gaze with a questioning look.

"You may kill me, but Lucian will hunt you down. He won't let my death go unavenged."

"No, he wouldn't." Lucian's cold voice sounded above them right before he yanked Kraid off of her. He swiped a clawed hand across Kraid's chest, ripping tendons and flesh, before sending his body flying twenty-five feet across the yard.

Rana scrambled to her feet and realized she was wet. She looked down. Her clothes and body were spattered with Kraid's blood. She glanced up in time to see Lucian leap across the distance between he and Kraid, landing hard on top of the vamp. But Kraid wasn't done. He slashed at Lucian's chest, shredding his clothes and skin. Lucian roared in anger and shoved his hand through Kraid's chest. Rana almost fainted at the sight and the sound of Kraid's screams of pain. Then nothing but eerie silence greeted her.

Rana looked down at her clothes, the blood. She could smell its metallic scent. She touched the sticky, warm moisture and her stomach turned when she realized she wondered what it tasted like.

No! she screamed in her mind. She fled back into the house, up the stairs and into her room. Tearing at the offending clothes, she couldn't get them off fast enough. She shivered as she stood beside the shower, waiting for the water to turn warm. Blood caked her hands and neck.

Rana stepped into the shower and grabbed the soap. Her hands trembling, her heart pounding, she rubbed the lather vigorously over her body. Off, off. She wanted the red stain off. The smell of death and now the appealing smell of life assailing her nostrils frightened her beyond measure.

Lucian materialized in the shower next to her. Reaching over, he grasped her wrists, staying her frantic movements. Rana met his unwavering pale silver gaze as the steam curled around them, wrapping them in a blanket of moist warmth.

Droplets of water glistened on his pitch-black hair as he took the soap from her hand and began bathing her body. Rana initially stiffened, but then closed her eyes and gave in to his ministrations. His gentle touch along her neck, shoulders and breasts worked to soothe her frazzled nerves.

She opened her eyes and ran her soapy hand over his chest, careful to avoid his wounds. She touched his neck and shoulders, covering all the firm planes of his body, appreciating his sculpted form. Never again to see him like this, to feel the hard, raw power underneath her hands. The thought tore at her heart. She committed his body to memory. Did one get to keep memories in heaven?

The warm water sluiced over her skin, washing away the blood and soap. Rana reveled in Lucian's fingers sliding over her. His large hands touched the curve of her hip, the indentation of her waist and trailed upward to her breasts, lifting them so he could kiss the pink tips one at a time. She gasped, closing her eyes when he sucked one of her taut nipples into his mouth, nipped at the tip, and then did the same to the other.

Rana moaned at his magical touch, putting her hands on his shoulders to steady herself. When Lucian wrapped his hands around her waist, she opened her eyes and her gaze landed on the ring on her finger, yanking her out of the seductive spell.

"I'm not Elizabeth, Lucian." She said stiffly. Dropping her hands, she backed up and looked away.

He stiffened. "Who told you—?" He paused. "Kraid."

Lucian cupped her face in his hands and turned her head so she had to meet his forceful gaze. "Rana, I know you're not Elizabeth. She may have been the reason I sought you, but you're my true mate."

She heard his words, but unbidden thoughts of the many times he could've told her about the ring and Elizabeth, but didn't, entered her mind. Her stomach churned with nausea, her chest tightened in pain.

"Here, take her ring…" She tried to pull off the ring, but even in the shower, with soapy hands, the ring wouldn't budge.

"Damn it all!" she yelled her frustration.

Lucian's big hand wrapped around hers, closing her hand into a fist. "No," he said angrily and set her back against the shower wall.

Rana gasped at the cold feeling of the tile pressed against her back. She lifted her chin and glared at him.

His infuriated silver gaze locked with hers. "I know the difference, Rana. I admire your courage and your compassion. I love your quick humor and strong sense of self." When she didn't respond, he clasped her arms in his hands and shook her gently, his jaw tight. "Elizabeth wasn't near as stubborn as you are. And I didn't have this all-consuming need to have her like I do you. You are my true mate. Get used to it."

Lucian didn't wait for a response. He pulled her to him, crushing her lips in a bruising, dominating kiss, his tongue invading her mouth. His intemperate desire fueled her own. Rana wrapped her arms around his neck and kissed him back, needing his touch, his connection. Her heart sang. His actions, even more than his words, told her he truly cared for *her*, not a woman from a lifetime ago.

His hand slid between then, cupping her breast, rubbing her nipple before sliding lower, seeking her swollen, throbbing clitoris. Rana moaned and pressed against him when his fingers found their mark. Sliding two fingers inside her, he tested her readiness and groaned against her mouth.

Rana grasped his shoulders and rose on tiptoe to give him easier access. He trailed kisses down her throat, grazing her neck with his teeth. Rana stiffened at the contact and he lifted his head.

"I'm trying to save you." She sighed. When he looked at her strangely, she amended saying, "Don't you need your energy for tonight?"

Lucian shook his head and kissed her jaw. Sliding his tongue down her neck, he ground out, "You're torturing me."

She moaned and wrapped her arms around his neck as he clasped her ass in his hands and lifted her against him. This time the cool tile didn't faze her when Lucian sank his hard shaft into her in one long driving stroke.

"You feel so good," he mumbled against her neck and then withdrew and thrust back in once more. "I will never get enough of you. Ever."

Rana tried to wrap her legs around him, but their bodies were too slippery. Lucian chuckled and accommodated her by grasping the arch of either foot. Cupping her feet in his hands, pinning her bent knees underneath the brawn of his muscular arms, he drove upward and into her again.

She clutched his thick shoulders, arched her back and sucked in her breath at the full penetration the position allowed. Never in her life had she been so completely possessed, felt so utterly filled.

The drag of his erection within her inner walls, the grind of his body against her pubic bone, the friction, the building feverish pitch had her heart thudding in her chest, making her wonder if she just might faint from the erratic breaths she took to keep up with her pounding pulse and spiraling desire. And this connection with Lucian felt so wonderful, so right. She knew. She loved him with every fiber of her being.

Her orgasm slammed through her body in throbbing, pulsing waves of pleasure and she cried out, "Lucian, oh God, Lucian."

Lucian gave a rough groan against her neck, his own climax clearly upon him. "I love you, Rana. You're mine, all mine," he said fiercely before he plunged his teeth into her soft skin, causing her to scream in shuddering ecstasy, drowning out the sound of the shower splattering around them.

Chapter Ten

Lucian shut the shower off and lifted her in his arms. He sat down on a white cushioned chair in the bathroom, cradling her in his arms.

Why did she feel so tired? *Somebody slap me and wake me up, damnit!* But try as she might to rouse herself, her body was just too lethargic. Rana snuggled against his neck and succumbed to his gentle strokes with the soft towel against her skin and hair.

Lucian laid her on the bed, moved over to the wall, and turned a knob to dim the bright lights to a nice evening glow. Rana rolled over to face him when he climbed into bed and propped himself up on his elbow. She felt so languid and secure in his bed, the silk sheets wrapping her in their warmth. Sliding a hand underneath her cheek on the pillow, she made a sigh of contentment and smiled at his handsome face.

Lucian reached over and gently tucked a strand of her hair behind her ear, his gaze lingering on her cheek, following the path his fingers had taken.

"Do you want to tell me about her?" Rana asked softly.

He met her gaze for the briefest of seconds before resuming his exploration of her skin. His fingers skimmed her shoulders and down her arm, creating currents of desire across her sensitive flesh. "Elizabeth was also human. I met her at the opera. Our relationship was very different. My desire for her built over time."

"Did you love her?" She hated to ask, but in some ways she felt connected to this woman because of Lucian.

He stopped his movements and regarded her for a long moment before he answered, "Yes, I did. She was a good person. My love for her is stronger now than ever."

Rana's heart contracted at his revelation. She dropped her gaze to his neck so he wouldn't see the hurt his words elicited.

Lucian touched her cheek and then cupped her jaw in his hand, lifting her chin so her gaze met his once more. "Because if it weren't for Elizabeth, I never would have found you."

Rana blinked back the tears and swallowed to push away the lump that had formed in her throat at his endearing words.

He smiled. "But I don't want to talk about Elizabeth. I want to talk about us."

Us? Us! Oh, Lucian, there can be no us. Her heart broke at the loving look in his eyes, the desire banked behind those pools of mercury staring back at her.

At her silence, Lucian grasped her hand and lifted her palm to his lips. "I love you, Rana. I want you to be my wife, my vampire mate."

Stall for time. Come on, think, Rana. "Lucian, I just don't know if I'm ready. I mean, the thought of drinking someone else's blood makes me nauseous." *That was pretty good and I didn't even have to lie. The idea does make me want to yark my guts up. Hey, Gatekeeper, you listening out there? I'm being a good girl down here.*

I'd like to know your definition of good girl, Rana, Jack said with a laugh. *Riding that fine line, aren't you?*

Rana snorted inwardly. *Jack, which way did you go? Up or down? Because I* know *you aren't being holier-than-thou with me, oh smoozmeister of all women.*

Lucian chuckled against her hand, making her think he'd read her thoughts until he laced his fingers with hers and said, "Rana, love, you'll get your sustenance from me and no other."

That got her attention. Rana sat up on her elbow as excitement coursed through her. The idea of sucking on his neck had an entirely different connotation. But wait? Something didn't compute. "Wait a minute. Though I don't find the idea of dining on you near as unappealing, where are you going to get your food?"

He shrugged. "The same way I always have, from humans."

She arched her eyebrow. "Women?"

Lucian grinned at her.

"I don't think so, Luc." She pushed him over on his back and sprawled across his chest. "Men only. Got it."

He laughed outright at her decree and then sobered. "Say it again, Rana. I like the way my name sounds on your lips."

"Luc." Rana smiled and curled into him, snuggling her back against his chest.

Lucian pulled her hair back and kissed her neck while his hand traced down her side as if memorizing every curve of her body. Rana sighed at his magical touch. Her nipples tingled and her sex throbbed to life as his hand moved upward to cup her breast. He twisted the pebbled tip between his fingers before pinching it lightly. Rana gasped and arched against him, reveling in the rigid flesh that brushed insistently against her backside. Never had she been so in tune with another person. Nor had anyone made her feel as cherished and desired as Lucian did. When he pressed against her more intently as if he wanted to imprint himself on her, her desire for him only intensified.

His hand slid lower until he drew his finger between her damp curls, skimming past her swollen nub and delving inside her heated center. Rana arched wantonly against him, anticipation curling in her belly, her need so great to have him inside her, she slipped her hand between her legs and guided him home.

Lucian groaned in her ear as he thrust to the hilt. "You're a slice of heaven every time, Rana. God, every single time."

She smiled and was surprised when Lucian rolled onto his back and pulled her fully on top of him. But she didn't have time to ponder the new position as his hands roamed over her body while he drew in and out of her sheath with deliberate, measured movements.

Rana's breathing turned ragged when he slid a hand between her legs and rubbed her moisture around her clitoris, pressing against it while his fingers tweaked and twirled a taut nipple. Her body gave way to the sensual onslaught and Rana keened in pleasure as her climax washed over her.

Lucian kissed her neck and laid his hand over her beating heart for a long moment. Rana wasn't sure how he did it, but he stayed inside her as he sat them both up, slid off the bed, reached for her hands, and wrapped her fingers around the thick bedpost.

His entire body bracketed her in, for he kept his hands over hers on the post as he whispered in her ear, "I love you with all my heart."

She wanted to tell him she loved him back, but she just couldn't. Not when she'd be breaking his heart all over again before the dawn broke the sky. Instead, she silently spread her legs to accommodate him. Lucian traced his hands down her arms to her hips where he wrapped those long fingers and broad palms around her hips, holding her in place for his first, forceful thrust. Rana gasped in delight, her heart hammering as she gripped the post tighter, arching into his driving thrusts with counter ones of her own. She smiled when she received a growl of satisfaction from Lucian for her efforts.

"I won't take your blood until you wish it, Rana. I promise." Lucian rasped against her neck. With one hand covering hers on the post, Lucian took her other hand and lowered it to the nest of curls between her legs, causing her to moan her approval. His fingers guided hers, moving her hand over her clitoris as he drove into her again and again until their bodies glistened with their exertions.

When he came, Rana met his groans of exaltation with ones of her own until the only thing she heard was their mingled labored breathing and the fervent beating of her own heart against her chest. As her breathing slowed, she had to admit she missed that last little rush she got when he sank his teeth into her neck.

Lucian gathered her close for a few minutes, holding her tight before he withdrew and lifted her in his arms. He kissed her on the temple and laid her in the bed. Climbing in beside her, he pulled her back against his chest. Rana never remembered feeling so safe and secure in her life.

They dozed together for a while and Rana awoke with a start, looking at the clock. It was two in the morning. She turned to see Lucian laying there staring at her.

"Have you been watching me sleep?" she asked.

"Yes."

She pointed to the clock. "Lucian, get up and get dressed, you have to be at the meeting in half an hour."

He casually lay back on the bed and clasped his hands behind his head. "I'm not going."

"What!" Panic seized her. She sat up and looked at him. "What do you mean you aren't going?"

Lucian turned to her, his expression calm. "I will only take the Vité position with you by my side as my mate, my *anima*."

"*Anima*?" she asked, confused.

"Yes, my *anima*. My soul. Rana, you complete me." His silver eyes regarded her while he awaited her reaction.

What! Unfortunately someone else had beaten him to the punch. Her soul wasn't up for grabs. Now what was she going to do? "Lucian, that's crazy. The vampires need their leader, one who will keep order and discipline among the clans."

He smiled. "That's exactly right. I want them to have the best leader possible." He laced his fingers through hers and rubbed his thumb along her palm. His smoky gaze met hers as he continued, "I've waited too long for you. You're my number one priority, because without you I won't make a great leader."

Rana closed her eyes. *Here's hoping I won't tip the 'purity' scale with this big fat lie I'm about to tell. I just hope Lucian can forgive me.*

"Okay."

Lucian sat up, flashing a brilliant smile.

She held up her hand. "I'll become your mate, your *anima*, but only after the ceremony."

At his scowl, she crossed her arms over her naked breasts and held her ground. "Those are my terms."

He didn't look thrilled, but Rana pushed him out of the bed. "Hurry up and get some clothes on. We need to be downstairs in ten minutes."

He leapt from the bed and got dressed so fast he stood in front of her grinning triumphantly before she even made it to the bathroom.

"Oh, good grief, you show off," she grumbled, pushing past him. Lucian chuckled as she shut the door behind her.

* * * * *

Rana sat in a chair along a sidewall in the solarium conference room. Even though Lucian had insisted she sit next to him, she'd refused, explaining she wasn't his mate yet and would sit next to him when that time came. It hurt her too much to consider taking a position at the table when she'd so thoroughly lied to him.

She surveyed the cream colored walls and high ceiling with the beautifully etched glass skylight all along the center of the ceiling. The skylight surprised her considering the fact vampires couldn't abide the sun. *The glass is heavily tinted, love. So even during the day, only light shines through, not the sun's rays,* Lucian spoke in her mind.

Rana met Lucian's gaze and smiled. Somehow she knew he had designed this room. He might be a creature of the night, but he loved the light and lots of it.

Her gaze drifted to the men at the rich mahogany conference table. All the leaders were in attendance with the exception of Kraid, of course. Ian sat in as the Bruens' leader. Sabryn flanked Lucian's left side at the head of the table. His Uncle Vlad sat on the right.

Sabryn glanced around the table. "The first order of business is to officially cast your vote for Lucian as Vité. As our bylaws state, the vote must be unanimous. Please turn your crests to show your vote."

Rana watched as each clan leader set his MP3 sized crest encrusted disk on the table one at a time. Lucian had explained the process to her on the way to the meeting. Colored crest side up meant a yes vote, gold side up meant a no vote.

Yes. She smiled.

Yes. Her heart thumped in her chest.

Yes. She loved him.

Yes. I wish I could be your wife, Lucian, with all my heart.

It was Ian's turn to set down the Bruens disk. He started to lower it to the table when a loud crashing sound above their heads made all the leaders jump back, all except Lucian. He didn't move as if he'd expected the intrusion.

A man landed with a thud on top of the table, shards of glass from the skylight streaming down with him. He had pitch-black hair, a cruel mouth, and eyes so dark they looked black. He turned to face Lucian.

"Don't I get to vote on behalf of the Bruens, now that you've killed Kraid?" he sneered.

Lucian met his gaze with an unperturbed one. "You forfeited that right when you helped your brother kill the human, Drace. Kraid has already paid the price."

Drace's body shook with anger. "I refuse to be judged for killing a vampire hunter."

Lucian's voice remained calm, but forceful. "You aren't being judged for killing a vampire hunter, Drace. You're being judged for how you killed him. Killing in self-defense is one thing, but killing for the pure pleasure of it, I won't allow. You tortured the man."

Drace snorted. "It's no less than he would've done to me." He turned to the other clan leaders, pointing to Lucian. "Do you hear what this human-loving vampire is saying? How can you vote for someone that sides with an inferior race every chance he gets?"

The Arryn leader spoke, "Lucian, Drace does have a point. We can't embrace humans with open arms. They fear us. And when some fear, they attack."

Lucian slowly stood and addressed the leaders. "I'm not asking you to embrace humans with open arms. All I ask is that we learn to live in harmony with them." He looked pointedly at each clan leader. "I know many of you have human friends."

"Yeah, but what would they say if they knew you were vampires?" Drace cut in, addressing the other vampires.

Lucian continued in a smooth tone as if he hadn't been interrupted. "There will be those that condemn us, yes, but I know we each have examples of human friends who are aware of our vampire status and can see past our differences to the real person within." The men nodded their agreement with his statement. Lucian let his gaze land on Rana briefly. *I love you*, he whispered in her mind and planted an invisible kiss on her lips before he turned to Ian.

Rana's heart broke at his words.

"What's the Bruen clan's vote, Ian?"

Ian gave him a roguish grin and flipped the disk into the air toward the table. End over end it turned until it landed, skittering across the broken glass, hitting Drace's boot, crest side up.

Drace narrowed his eyes on Ian. "You can't vote for the Bruens."

Ian met his challenging gaze. "I can now, and my first order of business is to hunt you down." He glanced at his watch and gave Drace a humorless smile. "To be fair, I'll even give you an hour head start."

Drace ground his teeth in anger and then hissed at him before shape-shifting into a raven, his clothes dropping behind him as he flew out the way he came.

Rana returned her gaze to Lucian. He looked at her and smiled. Her heart soared for him. He seemed happy, fulfilled. The smile on his face brought a memory slamming back, a memory of Lucian dressed in clothes from the 1930's, smiling at her just like that. All the little things that had seemed familiar about him, the coffee, the way he looked at her, she knew. He *had* found her because of her connection to Elizabeth.

She sent a silent thank you to Elizabeth when The Gatekeeper suddenly appeared, standing right next to Lucian. Rana drew in her breath. Tonight the old man wore a flowing white robe, but he still had that red baseball cap perched on his head.

The Gatekeeper looked at her and nodded.

Her lungs started to contract and her chest burned with slicing pain. Spots formed in front of her eyes and her vision began to blur. She looked at Lucian and gasping though the waves of agony spoke to him in his mind, *I love you, Lucian*, right before she collapsed.

"Rana!"

She felt Lucian's arms around her, lifting her against his chest, heard the anguish and fear in his voice from far away as if he were speaking through a tunnel. "Hold on, Rana love."

Chapter Eleven

Cold fear trickled down Lucian's spine as he cradled Rana's limp body in his arms. *No, this can't be happening. She'd told me she loved me. I heard her.*

"Uncle Vlad, get Mora," he barked over his shoulder. He walked out of the room and vaulted up the stairs as fast as his vamp powers would let him. Once in his bedroom, with Rana cradled in his arms, he lay back against the headboard of his bed and looked down at her beautiful face.

Her closed eyes and furrowed brow indicated she was in pain. But she wasn't moaning and the silence scared him more than anything. He pressed his finger to her throat. Her pulse beat at an unsteady, sputtering rhythm.

He smoothed his hand over her head and down her hair. Somehow he sensed that Rana's life hung in uncertainty. "You can't leave me, Rana. I won't allow it," he said angrily.

Mora and Vlad entered the room and Lucian implored her as he lay Rana down on the bed, "Please help her, Mora. I can't lose my wife when I've just found her."

Lucian moved out of the way, so Mora could check Rana. He trusted her explicitly. She had years of experience with old vampire medicine. She checked Rana's pulse against her throat, looked at her pupils, listened to her heart.

"Her pulse is very weak." When she touched her fingers to Rana's throat once more, Mora quickly leaned near her mouth. She jerked up and said, "She's stopped breathing."

Lucian's heart thudded in his chest while she showed him how to elevate Rana's neck for CPR.

"Now, I'm going to press on her chest in three counts, after that you breathe for her, got it?"

Lucian nodded, his hands shaking as he waited for Mora to tell him to breathe for Rana. His stomach tightened in knots while they worked in unison to revive his mate, but after a few minutes, Mora put her hand on his arm.

"I'm sorry, Lucian."

Lucian set his jaw, his heart constricting in his chest at his loss. "Please leave us," he said quietly.

Vlad and Mora reluctantly left him, shutting the door behind them.

When the door clicked closed, Lucian climbed back into the bed and gathered Rana in his arms, holding her close. As he rocked her, her head fell back, her neck limp like a broken flower. He touched her hair, her face, and her neck. "No, Rana, you can't leave me. No."

Lucian finally let the emotions he'd held back for so many years punch through to the surface — anguish over waiting and wanting for so long, pain for the brief time they had together, and regret for the family they would never have. He kissed her forehead and accepted the emptiness as deep sorrow filled the void left open when he surrendered his long suppressed feelings.

"She came back for you."

Lucian jerked his head up and focused his gaze on the man standing at the end of the bed. He wore a flowing white robe and a bright light surrounded him. Lucian clutched Rana closer, wincing at the pain the brilliant light caused.

"Rana died from the car accident," the old man said. "I couldn't change that. I only bought her time so she could help you. But now I'm here to make it right." The old man looked at Rana, cradled in his arms. "Make her yours, Lucian. The child she carries is special. He possesses the psychic gift passed on from his mother. Raise him with your ideals in mind and keep your promise to rid the Kendrians of the evil that permeates it."

Before he could speak, the man vanished as quickly as he'd come.

Lucian lowered his hand to Rana's stomach in awe. *Our child.*

He looked at her beautiful face, her pale, flawless skin. He heard her breathing start anew, heard the slow, sluggish *whoosh* of her blood pushing through her veins once more.

"I love you, Rana."

Lucian touched her weak pulse with his lips and fed. Her blood was the sweetest of wines as the warm liquid flowed into him, thrumming through his body, feeding the fire he knew would never extinguish between them.

When he gingerly closed her wounds, Rana stirred and moaned, her eyes fluttering open. She put a limp hand on his arm and met his gaze. "Lucian? Where am I?"

He pulled her close and said huskily against her temple, "You're home, sweet Rana, you're home."

"But...but..."

"Shh," he said and ran his hand over her hair, soothing himself as much as her. "I want you to sleep now. We can talk later."

"Lucian…" she began.

"Sleep, my love," he compelled her.

Lucian watched her eyes drift closed, thankful for his ability to send her to sleep. He didn't want her to suffer through the painful metamorphosis her human body would have to undergo as she became a vampire.

* * * * *

Lucian walked into the library and saw Ian standing by the window and his sister and uncle each sitting in wing back chairs, waiting for him. Apparently the other vampire leaders had returned to their homes. Ian turned to him, concern in his eyes. Before he could ask, Lucian supplied the answer with a smile. "Rana is fine."

"What?" his uncle Vlad said, looking pleasantly surprised.

"But she's no longer human, is she?" Trish accused from the doorway. She glanced back toward the staircase and then returned her gaze to him, stating in a detached, matter-of-fact tone, "I heard her heart stop."

Lucian rubbed the back of his neck, hoping to release the tension that had taken over his body. Rana's whole miraculous recovery scenario was indeed beyond his comprehension. His mate may be fine now, but his body had been so tightly coiled throughout the whole ordeal, the bunched muscles in his neck and back would take more time to work themselves out.

He sighed. "It's a long story, but suffice it to say, Rana's my true mate now. I sent her to sleep during the change."

"So you saved her," Trish said, her words more of a statement than a question.

Lucian met her gaze. "No, she saved me."

Trish smiled. Apparently she liked his answer, for it was the first smile he'd seen on her face since she arrived. She turned and walked away without a word. He chuckled when he heard her mumble, "You're still all a bunch of freaks."

His uncle shook his head and looked at the empty doorway saying, "That one is going to give us a run for our money. I feel it in my bones." He turned to Lucian. "I'll let Mora know the good news concerning Rana."

Sabryn jumped up and hugged her brother tight around his neck. "I knew you'd find peace and happiness one day, Lucian. I'm so thrilled for you."

Lucian hugged her back and then set her away from him to look into her lilac colored eyes. "Now it's your turn, Sabryn. You deserve your own happiness."

Sabryn punched him in the arm. "Already trying to kick me out are you?"

"No, I—" He stopped mid sentence when he saw the devilish gleam in her eye. She'd deftly changed the subject, putting him on the defensive on purpose.

Before he could call her on her game she waved to their uncle. "Come on, Uncle Vlad. Let's leave Lucian and Ian to strategize on how best to hunt down Drace."

Lucian waited until Sabryn and his uncle left before he addressed Ian. "I want him eliminated yesterday, Ian."

Ian chuckled, always his laidback self. "No worries, Luc. I'll get Drace."

Lucian met his golden gaze. "Whatever it takes, my friend. Getting Drace will help establish your role as the new Bruen leader." Then a thought occurred to him that might help Ian out, too. How many times had Ian told him of his brother's self imposed seclusion? "Why don't you ask Duncan to help? What better way to accomplish your goal of bringing your brother into both the human and the vampire world than for him to become a vampire hunter?"

"You do have a valid point." Ian grinned as he sat down. That's an angle I hadn't considered with my brother. But Drace is mine, Luc. I'll handle him myself. As for Duncan, it'll have to be just the right kind of case or he'll smell my efforts and take the exact opposite course."

Lucian nodded. "I'll leave the timing up to you then, but you may need some additional help since you'll have other responsibilities to fulfill as the Bruen leader."

Ian rolled his eyes and said, "What have I gotten myself into?"

Lucian laughed, enjoying the rich, hearty feeling in his chest. It felt so good to really laugh again. "Welcome to my world."

* * * * *

Rana awoke to the sound of Lucian closing the door. She noted her naked state underneath the covers as she lifted her head and looked at the clock.

"Is it really eight o'clock in the evening?"

Lucian nodded as he stripped out of his navy blue sweater. Rana's heart thudded against her ribs at the sight of his broad, muscular chest. She closed her eyes briefly and inhaled his scent. Even from across the room, she could smell the exotic aroma that was all Lucian.

He slipped out of his pants, stripping his silk boxers with them and turned toward the bed, his erection hard and proud, bouncing against his lower stomach. Rana drew in her breath at his magnificent body. She'd never tire of looking at him.

Wait a minute. Wasn't she supposed to be dead? As Lucian approached, she heard his heart pounding, the rush of his blood as it coursed through his veins. The sound made her realize how incredibly thirsty she was. *Okay, that's a bit on the freaky side. The idea of rushing blood should make me nauseous, that is unless I'm a....*

"Lucian?"

Lucian lay down beside her and propped himself up on his elbow while he gently pushed her onto her back. "Yes, love?" He leaned over her and ran his hand down her neck and collarbone and then skimmed his fingers over her breast.

She grabbed his wrist before he could continue his downward path and heard his heart beat trip in his chest. "Am I a vampire?"

Lucian smiled and kissed her forehead. "Yes, love, you are. It appears you were given a second chance at life — a life with me."

"But I was supposed to die." Happiness and confusion warred within her.

Lucian pulled his wrist from her loosened grasp and clasped her hand in his. Sliding their hands lower, he splayed her fingers over her lower belly, covering her hand with his larger one.

"You have a reason to live other than for us, sweet Rana."

Rana jerked her gaze back to his silver one.

He smiled. "You carry our child. The next Vité." He chuckled. "And apparently he's going to be quite special according to an angel friend of yours."

She smiled. "A child?"

Our child, he answered in her mind and brought her hand to his lips.

Rana gave him a seductive smile and pulled his hand to her mouth. She returned the favor, kissing his fingers, but instead of letting his hand go, she put her lips around his finger, sucking it into her mouth.

Lucian's breathing changed, blatant desire reflected in his eyes as he watched her. When she sat up and straddled his hips, running her hands up his chest, he leaned back against the headboard and growled his approval.

"You're all mine," she said and gave her own growl of appreciation as she slid her warm, moist entrance along his hard length.

Lucian grasped her waist in his hands, lifted her, and placed his erection against her hot core before thrusting hard and deep into her, touching her womb inside.

She gasped in delight at the pain-pleasure she experienced as his shaft forced her body to immediately adjust to his size and length.

Lucian's expression turned to one of concern. "The baby?"

"Is just fine," she finished with a smile and she began to rock against his hard body.

At her seductive pace, he inhaled deeply, "God, you feel so good. I could stay buried in you for a week."

"How about for a few centuries." Rana grinned at him as she rose up on her knees and then sat back down, taking him fully inside once more, causing him to groan his satisfaction. The glide of his hard shaft deep within her made her shudder in excited anticipation. Her vampire heart couldn't keep up with her spiraling emotions. It thumped slowly underneath her ribcage, heightening her arousal, making her want to know what it would take to make her heart beat harder. Lucian's strong hands clamped around her waist and guided her movements, feeding the coiled tension burning within her.

She kissed his neck, reveling in his ragged breathing, and the upward thrust of his hips against hers. He smelled spicy and clean and totally aroused. The scents and the sound of his pumping heart and racing blood only heightened her desire. Her nostrils flared and the strange sensation of her canines lengthening made her feel so totally out of control she paused her movements.

Before she could pull back, Lucian clasped a firm hand on the back of her neck while he drove into her. "Feed, Rana," he rasped out the order.

Rana moaned at the pleasure his powerful thrust caused and slid her teeth into his throat. Lucian gave a low growl and climaxed as she fed, his pistoning thrusts sending her over the edge right along with him. His blood tasted so heady and powerful, she wanted more, more. Her mind had a hard time deciding which satisfied her more, his blood coursing down her throat or the delicious climax she'd just experienced with him.

When her thirst abated, she reluctantly pulled away, licking the wounds closed on his neck. Gazing into his silver eyes she asked, "Is it always like that when you feed? So incredibly, emotionally erotic?"

Lucian drew a finger along her cheek and jaw line. "No. Only with your *anima* is it like this, Rana love."

Rana gave him a stern look. "Good, because I was beginning to wonder if you feeding on men would be a problem for me, too."

Lucian chuckled and reached over to pull something from the nightstand drawer. He leaned back against the headboard, turned her around and gathered her in his arms. Settling her back against his chest, he lifted her hand and touched the ring on her finger. Rana stared in awe as he effortlessly slid the piece of jewelry off her hand.

"How did you do that...?" she started to ask.

"Magic," he chuckled in her ear as he added a thin band to the ring and slid it back on.

Where there had been a teardrop opening at the top of the ring, a single pear shaped diamond now nestled in its space right in the middle of the two blood red pear shaped rubies.

She held up her hand and the stones glittered in the light. "It finally looks complete." She sighed.

"And so am I," Lucian said as he wrapped his arms around her and kissed her neck. Running his thumb over the ring, he said, "Now you have a part of me and a part of you."

Rana's heart contracted in her chest as her excitement grew. She glanced up at him. "The diamond? Is it really from my tear?"

He nodded.

Her sluggish heart beat faster. She looked back at the ring. "And the rubies?"

"Are my blood."

Lucian laced his fingers with hers. *Tears and blood, Rana love. I think we've shed enough, don't you?*

Her heart soared at his words. Rana snuggled into his warmth, appreciating the secure feeling of his strong arms around her. She kissed his hand and smiled. A life with Lucian and their child. *I love you with all my heart,* she whispered in his mind. *And yes, I believe we've both paid our dues.*

About the author:

Born and raised in the southeast, Patrice Michelle has been a fan of romance novels since she was thirteen years old. Though she enjoys reading many types of books, from mysteries to sci-fi, she has always come back to romances, saying, "There's just something about a sexy happy-ever-after that gets to me every time."

Patrice has always preferred reading sensual romances and when she started writing, all her stories leaned toward the erotic. Writing both paranormal and contemporary romantica books for Ellora's Cave has given her the freedom to let her imagination run free, to push the envelope to her heart's content.

She enjoys spending time with her family and friends, reading, photography, and writing, lots of writing.

Patrice loves to hear from readers. Email her anytime at patrice@patricemichelle.net.

Patrice Michelle welcomes mail from readers. You can write to her c/o Ellora's Cave Publishing at P.O. Box 787, Hudson, Ohio 44236-0787.

Why an electronic book?

We live in the Information Age—an exciting time in the history of human civilization in which technology rules supreme and continues to progress in leaps and bounds every minute of every hour of every day. For a multitude of reasons, more and more avid literary fans are opting to purchase e-books instead of paperbacks. The question to those not yet initiated to the world of electronic reading is simply: *why?*

1.*Price.* An electronic title at Ellora's Cave Publishing runs anywhere from 40-75% less than the cover price of the <u>exact same title</u> in paperback format. Why? Cold mathematics. It is less expensive to publish an e-book than it is to publish a paperback, so the savings are passed along to the consumer.

2.*Space.* Running out of room to house your paperback books? That is one worry you will never have with electronic novels. For a low one-time cost, you can purchase a handheld computer designed specifically for e-reading purposes. Many e-readers are larger than the average handheld, giving you plenty of screen room. Better yet, hundreds of titles can be stored within your new library—a single microchip. (Please note that Ellora's Cave does not endorse any specific brands. You can check our website at *www.ellorascave.com* for customer recommendations we make available to new consumers.)

3.*Mobility.* Because your new library now consists of only a microchip, your entire cache of books can be taken with you wherever you go.

4.*Personal preferences are accounted for.* Are the words you are currently reading too small? Too large? Too...ANNOYING? Paperback books cannot be modified according to personal preferences, but e-books can.

5.*Innovation.* The *way* you read a book is not the only advancement the Information Age has gifted the literary community with. There is also the factor of *what* you can read. Ellora's Cave Publishing will be introducing a new line of interactive titles that are available in e-book format only.

6.*Instant gratification.* Is it the middle of the night and all the bookstores are closed? Are you tired of waiting days—sometimes weeks—for online and offline bookstores to ship the novels you bought? Ellora's Cave Publishing sells instantaneous downloads 24 hours a day, 7 days a week, 365 days a year. Our e-book delivery system is 100% automated, meaning your order is filled as soon as you pay for it.

Those are a few of the top reasons why electronic novels are displacing paperbacks for many an avid reader. As always, Ellora's Cave Publishing welcomes your questions and comments. We invite you to email us at service@ellorascave.com or write to us directly at: P.O. Box 787, Hudson, Ohio 44236-0787.

Printed in the United States
19817LVS00005B/1-84